Rushed

OTHER BOOKS BY AURORA ROSE REYNOLDS

The Until Series

Until November

Until Trevor

Until Lilly

Until Nico

Second Chance Holiday

Until Her Series

Until July

Until June

Until Ashlyn

Until Harmony

Until December

Until April (coming soon)

Until Him Series

Until Jax

Until Sage

Until Cobi

Until Talon

Shooting Stars Series

Fighting to Breathe

Wide-Open Spaces

One Last Wish

Underground Kings Series

Assumption

Obligation

Distraction

Infatuation

Ruby Falls Series

Falling Fast

One More Time

Fluke My Life Series

Running into Love

Stumbling into Love

Tossed into Love

Drawn into Love

How to Catch an Alpha Series

Catching Him

Baiting Him

Hooking Him

Stand-Alone Novels

Love at the Bluebird

The Wrong/Right Man

Alpha Law (written as C. A. Rose)

Justified (written as C. A. Rose)

Liability (written as C. A. Rose)

Finders Keepers (written as C. A. Rose)

To Have to Hold to Keep Series

Trapping Her

Taking Her (coming soon)

Stalking Her (coming soon)

Rushed

Adventures in Love, Book One

AURORA ROSE
REYNOLDS

This is a work of fiction. Names, characters, organizations, places, events, and incidents are either products of the author's imagination or are used fictitiously.

Published by Montlake, Seattle

www.apub.com

ISBN-13: 9781542034548
ISBN-10: 154203454X

Cover design by Hang Le

Cover photography by Regina Wamba of MaeIDesign.com

Printed in the United States of America

Rushed

Chapter 1

Cybil

I enter Stone's bar and head toward the back, scanning the space for Jade and trying to ignore the stares and whispers even as my cheeks warm with humiliation. When I see her wave from across the room, the tension in my shoulders loosens slightly, and I quicken my steps.

"Are you okay?" she asks carefully as I slide into the booth, take off my wide-brimmed floppy hat, and place it on the seat next to my suede bag.

"This is the first time I've been here since . . ." My words trail off, and understanding fills her eyes before she looks around. When her brows drag together and her full lips form a frown, I know everyone is now watching us.

"What the hell is wrong with people?" she asks a little too loudly, making me cringe.

"It's fine. It's just going to take some time before I'm old news," I whisper, grabbing her hand to gain her attention.

"It's ridiculous that your broken engagement is the only thing people have to talk about," she grumbles, and I press my lips together. She's not wrong, but then again, I've lived in this town my entire life. When my mom passed away, the people here looked out for me. They watched me grow up, knew when I fell in love, cheered me on when

I got engaged to my high school sweetheart, and were planning on attending my wedding in just a couple of months.

Maybe not all of them, but a lot of them.

"Once they see I'm okay, things will go back to normal," I assure her and maybe myself.

"It would be easier for everyone to see that you're okay if you weren't hiding away in your shop all the damn time."

"I'm not hiding; I'm working," I say with a sigh.

Okay, I've also been hiding, but who can blame me for needing some time? One minute I was laying out seating arrangements for my wedding dinner, and the next, Galvin, my now-ex-fiancé, was telling me that he didn't want to get married anymore. Worse, he didn't even have a reason. The only thing he kept saying was, "It's not you; it's me." I still don't know what the hell that even means.

I shake away those thoughts and the reminder of him. "With my trip to Montana tomorrow, I needed to get all my orders ready and shipped out."

"A trip you didn't even want." She shakes her head. "I still think you should tell Galvin that he needs to pay you back, at least for his half."

"It was a gift." I let out a breath and fiddle with my napkin, wondering if he knew he wanted to end things four months ago, when he started talking about us going on a couples retreat to strengthen our relationship. I thought we were solid but figured two weeks in Montana with just the two of us wouldn't hurt, so I booked us a long trip with Live Life Adventures. I even added a few extra days to the end to just relax and take in some of the sights between Oregon and Montana.

"It's also ridiculous that you can't get a refund, given that you're no longer actually going on a couples retreat."

"It's nonrefundable. I knew that when I signed the contracts."

"Whatever." She rolls her eyes.

"It will be fine, and honestly, I'm looking forward to the time away."

"Camping and hiking?" She raises a brow.

"Okay, so neither of those things are exactly my idea of a good time, but who knows—maybe I'll end up loving them. And really, I just need to get out of town for a while. I want to go somewhere people don't know my sob story."

"I wish I didn't have to work so I could go with you."

"I know, but I get that you can't just close down your store for two weeks," I tell her as I tip my head back to look at Connie, the owner of Stone's, when she stops at the edge of our table.

"Jade," she says; then her eyes come to me and fill with pity as her voice drops to just above a whisper. "Cybil, you doing okay, honey?"

"I'm good, Connie. Thank you." I smile, which makes her look even more concerned. Wanting the awkwardness to be over, I pick up the menu and scan it quickly. "I think I'll have the french onion soup and a Diet Coke."

"I'll have the same and two lemon drops, please."

"Sure." She looks like she wants to say more but thinks better of it. "I'll be right back with your drinks." She walks off, jotting down our order on her notepad.

"Two lemon drops?" I raise a brow at my best friend.

"What? We deserve a fucking drink." She rolls her eyes, then adds, "Or at least *you* deserve a drink."

"Right." I shake my head. "I'm only having one drink. Tomorrow I have a fourteen-hour drive, and I don't want to be hungover."

"Mom and Dad are flipping out that you're driving alone."

"Believe me, they have both shared that they are not happy with me." I roll my eyes. Maisie and Bernard, Jade's parents, were two of my mom's closest friends when she was alive. When she was diagnosed with cancer, they were there every step of the way. Then, when she passed, they took me in and loved me like their own. I love them to the bottom of my soul, but they really frustrate me when they treat me like a kid instead of a twenty-six-year-old woman.

"I'm also worried about it."

"I'll be fine." I give her a reassuring smile. "I promise I'll be safe, and I already loaded up on car snacks and drinks, so I won't have to stop too often."

"Just promise me that you won't stop at sketchy rest stops when you have to use the restroom."

"Promise," I agree easily, then lean back when our drinks arrive.

When she picks up her lemon drop and holds it up, I do the same. "To new starts."

"To new starts." I clink my glass with hers, then shoot back the sweet-and-sour liquid that warms my stomach and relaxes me for the rest of dinner. When we finish eating and pay our tab, we head outside to the parking lot, stopping at my car since it's closer.

"I'm going to miss you." She pulls me in for a hug, and I hold her tightly, unsure where I would be without her support these last few weeks. Really these last few years.

"I'll be back in two weeks."

Keeping hold of my arms, she leans back and locks her eyes with mine. "I can't wait to hear every detail when you get home, but promise you'll call."

"I'll call you every chance I get." My throat gets tight as I fight back tears. "I love you."

She pulls me in for another hug. "I love you too. Try to have fun."

"I'll try," I agree as she lets me go, wiping her eyes as she steps away.

"Just don't do anything wild like fall in love with one of those Montana guys."

Laughing, I shake my head. "I guarantee you that is not going to happen. No more men for me."

Her face softens, and her head tips to the side. "Galvin isn't who you were meant to be with, Cybil, and I think deep down you know that, given some of the things that happened in your relationship," she says, and my stomach twists because I know she's right. "It just sucks, because you've always thought of him when you've imagined your future, but he's not who you're supposed to be with. You'll find your guy when you least expect it."

I give her the nod I know she's waiting for, and she shakes her head before spinning on her heel and heading for her car, shouting over her shoulder, "You'll see! Your Prince Charming is out there waiting for you."

Laughing, I get into my Bronco and start the engine. I'm not sure about Prince Charming, but I do know I have two weeks ahead of me that are going to push me out of my comfort zone, and that might be just what I need right now.

Chapter 2

Cybil

Covering my mouth as I yawn, I glance down at my GPS and see I'm only about five minutes from the hotel I booked myself for the night. I drive through a town that looks a lot like the one I grew up in, with cute little shops lining the street, and scan the road on each side. I'm looking for somewhere to stop and get something in my stomach before I go find my bed for the evening.

I pass by a couple of fast-food places but keep going, knowing they probably won't have anything for me to eat besides french fries, and sadly those crunchy bits of heaven won't cut it tonight. After turning around at the end of town, I decide to head down one of the busy-looking side roads off the main drag, then spot the sign for a bar and grill off in the distance. Not seeing a space, I pass the restaurant and start scanning the road for a place to park, then sigh in relief when I spot an older woman getting into her car.

I flip on my turn signal and pull down my visor to check my reflection. After rubbing away the dark smudges of mascara under my eyes, I flip the mirror back into place, then watch in disbelief as a huge truck curves around me to angle into the space I've been waiting for. Tired, hungry, and now annoyed, I pull forward with my finger hovering over my passenger-window button, ready to roll it down and give the driver a piece of my mind for stealing my spot, but I stop as a man unfolds from the truck.

Boot-covered feet hit the ground first. Long legs encased in denim and a torso covered in a dark-green tee with a long-sleeved plaid over it that fits tight across his abs, muscular chest, and biceps follow. Then *him*. My breath gets caught in my throat when I get a glimpse of his profile: a strong jaw covered in stubble and a nose straight off a Greek god statue. Which, along with his full lips and dark hair that appears almost black in the light of the setting sun, has me stunned.

When he disappears around the hood of his truck, I shake myself out of my daze and drive forward, reminding myself there are literally millions of good-looking men in the world, including my ex, and most of them are not worth the dirt they kick up with their boots. After driving up and down past the restaurant twice, I finally find a place to park and get out.

I grab my bag off the passenger seat and head inside, trying not to feel awkward when I see that most of the people are here to meet others or are hanging out in groups. Holding my purse close to my hip, I wait in the line that's formed near the front door, trying to ignore the looks coming my way. With most of the women wearing jeans and T-shirts, I must stand out in my loose cream lace tank, bell-bottomed jeans, wedge heels, floppy hat, and fringed vegan leather bag I designed and hand-stitched each and every detail onto.

When I finally reach the front of the line, I step up to the podium, smiling at the redhead who's been seating everyone, and blink when she looks over my shoulder without even acknowledging me.

"Hey, Tanner." A megawatt smile curves her full lips, making her even prettier than she already is. "Are you wanting a table?"

"Yeah, thanks," a deep voice rumbles behind me, and I turn to look over my shoulder, narrowing my eyes when I see it's the guy who stole my parking spot earlier. Not that he notices. Like most people today, he's staring at his phone like it has the answers to life and barely looks up from it when he follows the hostess to a small table.

"Jerk." I glare at him as the redhead hands him a menu, which he accepts without even a thank-you. Not that she cares—her smile hasn't faltered once.

"Are you waiting to be seated?"

At that question, I focus on the older gentleman now standing behind the podium.

"Yes." I force a smile.

"Just one?" He looks down at the laminated table layout in front of him.

"Just one."

"It looks like it's going to be about ten more minutes for a table, but you can eat at the bar if you don't feel like waiting."

Instead of complaining, like Jade would do if she were here, I let out a breath and nod. "I'll just do that, thank you."

"You're welcome. Enjoy."

"Thanks." I head across the room, taking off my hat when I reach the bar. I find an empty seat at the end and climb up onto one of the stools, smiling at the bartender when he starts walking my way. Excited that I'm finally going to get something to eat, I turn to set my bag on the stool next to me, and when I spin around, Tanner—with his broad shoulders and thick hair—is leaning into the bar at my side, holding a ten-dollar bill between his fingers.

"Mason," he calls out, and the bartender lifts his chin in acknowledgment. "Let me get a Miller."

"Are you kidding me right now?" I bite out, not even attempting to hide my annoyance, and he turns his head my way. When his hazel eyes lock with mine, he blinks. "Am I invisible?"

"Pardon?" He shakes his head, causing a chunk of hair to fall over his brow.

"Am I invisible?" I repeat, ignoring the way my fingers twitch, wanting to push that piece of hair away from his forehead. "I'm just asking because this is the third time you've cut me off, so either I'm invisible, or you're just a jerk."

"I haven't cut you off," he denies, standing to his full height, which means I have to tip my head way, way back to keep our eyes locked.

"You did! You stole my parking spot, you stole my table, and now you're stealing my bartender."

"Your bartender?" he repeats, and I narrow my eyes.

"I was here first, so yes. *My* bartender."

"I didn't see you." He runs his fingers through his hair.

"So I am invisible." I roll my eyes and grab the menu from the little holder on the bar . . . and get more annoyed when I see it's nothing but drinks.

"Everything okay here, Tanner?" the bartender asks, handing him the beer he asked for as his gaze pings between the two of us.

"Just a little miscommunication," Tanner says. "Can you put whatever she wants on my bill?"

"I'm not drinking. I'm eating." I glare at him, then look at the bartender and plaster a sweet smile on my face. "I don't want him to pay for my food, but can I please see a menu?"

"Sure." He smirks at Tanner as he reaches under the counter, pulls one out, and hands it to me. "I'll give you a few minutes to look it over. Just shout for me when you're ready. My name's Mason."

"Thank you, Mason."

"Anytime." He winks and I sigh, dropping my eyes to look over the menu while ignoring the man at my side, who I can feel still watching me.

"Look," Tanner says, resting his elbows on the bar and bringing us closer together. "I feel bad about what happened. I was distracted, but I swear I didn't do any of that shit on purpose."

"It's fine," I mumble, wishing he would go away, because the scent of pine, leather, and *him* is starting to play with my head.

"You're saying it's fine, but I'm getting the feeling it's not. Please, let me buy you dinner."

"No, thank you."

"A drink then," he says, and I turn, coming face to face with him. Damn, up close, he's seriously difficult to look at he's so perfect. "One drink." He holds his hands together like he's praying.

"You can pay for my lemonade," I say, giving in, and he grins, showing off straight white teeth and a dimple in his scruff-covered cheek.

"You ready to order?" Mason comes back, and I'm more than a little thankful for the distraction.

"I'll have a lemonade, the vegetable quesadilla, and a bowl of pumpkin soup."

"You got it, babe." He goes to the computer on the counter to type something in, then pours my drink from the machine on the back wall.

"I'm covering her drink and my beer." Tanner hands him the ten he's still holding while Mason gives me my drink along with a straw. Ignoring the straw, I start to take a sip but end up looking at Tanner over the rim of the glass. I raise a brow when I find him still watching me.

"You're not from around here."

"I'm not," I agree, and he smiles again, which he needs to stop doing, because it's making me find him even more attractive.

"Tanner, your food!" someone shouts from across the room, and he looks that way briefly before turning his attention back to me.

"Well, it was nice meeting you, sunshine. Maybe I'll see you around."

"Probably not." I shrug, and that dimple of his gets a little deeper before he stands to his full height and saunters to his table. I wish I could say I don't watch him go, but I do, and when he's seated, he turns to look at me over his shoulder, a smug smile tilting up the corners of his mouth. I roll my eyes and turn back to face the bar, trying to figure out what the strange feeling in the pit of my stomach is.

Chapter 3

Cybil

"Are you nervous?" Jade asks, her voice echoing through my phone's speaker as I pull onto a dirt road that should lead me to the Live Life Adventures Lodge, where I'm meeting my guide this morning.

"Yes, I'm also sure that I'm going to end up toppling over under the weight of my backpack, which should be fun." I smile when she laughs.

"Didn't they send you a list of stuff to pack?"

"They did, but they told me that I should add anything else I might need, so I might have gone overboard with books, granola bars, and extra clothes."

"Why am I not surprised?"

"Because you know me," I say, then breathe "No" when the lodge comes into view and I see none other than Tanner standing out front. There are two other men dressed just like him in a uniform of cargo pants, T-shirts with the Live Life Adventures logo on the chest, and boots on their feet, the three of them tall, broad, and good looking. One with dirty-blond hair, a sun-kissed tan, and tattoos traveling up one of his arms, the other with short jet-black hair and obvious native ancestry that makes him look fierce yet regal, which is a beautiful combination.

"What?" Jade asks as all eyes turn to watch me drive by.

"Nothing. I'm here." I park my Bronco as my stomach dances with a new type of nervousness.

"Oh, okay. Well, I love you."

"Love you too. I'll call when I can."

"Be safe."

"I will." I hang up while I shut down the engine, then take a breath and open the door to get out. When my seat belt stops me, I grimace, then quickly release the lock and hop out of my seat.

"Hey, sunshine," Tanner calls out as I walk toward the trunk.

I rub my hands down the front of my black leggings as I lock eyes with him. "Umm." I glance from him to the other two men, feeling my cheeks warm when I find them studying me. "I'm here for the couples retreat."

"The couples retreat?" He looks over my shoulder, his eyes narrowing before they come back to me. "Where's your partner?"

"I'm alone." I shrug while making an *eek!* face. "I guess I should have booked this retreat for a few months ago."

"Shit," the blond guy at his side mutters.

"You're Cybil?" the other man asks, and I nod. "I'm Maverick. We spoke a couple of times. Sorry about your breakup."

"It happens," I say awkwardly as the blond mutters another curse.

"You can leave your bag in your trunk for now and go on inside the lodge, where everyone else is. Tanner, Blake, and I will be there in just a couple of minutes to go over the plans for the next week."

"Everyone else?" I frown.

"The other couples," Tanner states, and I blink.

"Other couples?"

"It's a couples retreat."

"Yeah, I know, but I thought . . ." I shake my head. "I didn't know there would be other couples. I thought my ex and I were the couple."

Maverick's lips twitch. "There are three couples on this retreat with you."

"Oh." I fiddle with the knot of the checkered red flannel I tied around my waist.

"Tanner's leading the retreat, so you'll be partnering up with him for all planned activities," he says, and my stomach drops to my toes. "You'll be in good hands."

"Sure." I quickly glance at Tanner, my chest beating oddly when I find him smiling. "I guess I'll just go inside."

"There's coffee and doughnuts. Help yourself."

"Okay, thanks." I walk past them and start up the wide steps that lead to the porch, stumbling over my stupid chunky hiking boots. Thankfully, I catch myself before I fall on my face, but I'm seriously wondering if I'm going to survive the next week between my pack, books, and now Tanner.

"You okay?"

Knowing it's Tanner who's asked, I don't even bother looking behind me. I raise my chin and wave a hand out as I clear the last step and walk toward the door. "Yep, never been better."

"You know the rules," I hear one of the guys say as I enter the lodge, but I don't hear more, because the sound of people chatting and laughing rings in my ears as I walk down a short hall. When I enter the great room, I realize the photos online didn't do it justice. It's beautiful, with high ceilings, exposed wood, and large picture windows that look out over the forest of tall ponderosa pines and gorgeous Douglas firs. The chatting of the couples seated on the two couches comes to a standstill as everyone turns to look at me, and I feel more awkward than I did before.

"Hi." I wave, glancing through everyone. "I'm Cybil."

"Nice to meet you, Cybil." A slim older gentleman with thinning hair and a kind smile stands, and the much younger, very pretty blonde woman he was sitting next to follows close behind. "I'm Dr. Oliver Price."

"And I'm his girlfriend." The blonde now plastered to his side flops out her hand toward me. "Lauren."

"Nice to meet you both." I smile at the two of them, then turn my attention to an attractive man with dark hair and thick black-rimmed glasses, and he grins at me.

"I'm Jacob," he greets, then nods to the equally attractive man at his side, who is smiling.

"I'm his husband, Parker. Come sit down." Parker motions to a chair that's kitty-corner to the couches that are facing each other. I step deeper into the room as everyone takes their seats, and I notice a third couple on the couch, holding up a phone and talking to a kid, judging by the way they're speaking.

"That's Grant and Avery. They're talking to their son," Parker tells me as I sit, and the man who must be Grant waves, then nudges his wife's shoulder and motions in my direction when she looks at him.

As she looks around the phone she's still holding up, her eyes meet mine. "Sorry, I'm Avery."

"Cybil," I greet, and she smiles.

"It's nice to meet you."

"You too," I reply as the child on the phone shouts *"Mom!"* making her sigh and focus on the phone once more.

"Where's your partner?" Lauren asks while she does that annoying thing some women do, where you know they are judging and dissecting each and every little detail about you.

"She's with me," Tanner says, walking into the room carrying a handful of papers, which he begins to pass out, while Maverick flips on the TV hanging on the wall, and Blake takes a seat in the chair next to mine. Taking one when he holds it out to me, I startle slightly when he sits on the arm of my chair. "The sheet of paper you're now holding has a breakdown of our daily itinerary. As you can see, every day, you'll be required to complete one task with your partner's help and—"

"Um, is that fair?" Lauren cuts in, holding up her paper. "If you're her partner, she's going to always win, because this is your job."

"I don't think this is a competition," Parker says, sounding annoyed, and Jacob presses his lips together like he's trying not to laugh.

"You're right; this is not a competition," Blake says as he stands. "The point of this retreat is to build trust between you and your partner. No relationship works unless you are able to work together, and—"

"Sorry," Lauren interrupts again, and everyone focuses on her. "I'm just wondering why she's here, if this is supposed to be a retreat for couples."

"Lauren," Oliver hisses, turning to glare at her.

"What? It's just a question." She frowns back.

"I'm here because I booked this trip for my fiancé and me, and since he's now my *ex*, he obviously didn't come," I say, figuring I might as well get it over with.

"Oh," Lauren whispers, while everyone else around the room shifts uncomfortably. "Sorry."

"No problem." I look up when a heavy hand rests on my shoulder and lock eyes with Tanner. He doesn't say anything, but then again, he doesn't have to. His expression tells me that he feels bad for me, which flipping sucks. I'm tired of people feeling sorry for me, tired of the pity-filled looks and awkwardness. I wanted to come on this trip to forget about the last couple of months, not to relive them.

"Now that *that's* out of the way, let's go over the schedule for the week, talk about the safety guidelines, and then load up in the bus. There's about an hour drive to the first drop-off location," Maverick says, holding the remote toward the TV, and the schedule on the paper I'm holding comes up on the screen.

For the next hour and a half, I listen to Tanner, Blake, and Maverick speak, and as I watch the three of them interact, I realize they are more than just men who work together. There's something seamless about the way they work together. They're completely in sync, like they know each other inside and out, which makes me curious about their relationship.

"Are there any questions?" Blake asks when the safety video comes to an end, his attention directed at Lauren, who's asked a million questions and interrupted a dozen times.

"I don't think so," she says, and Oliver sighs, probably relieved that we can all finally move along.

"Then let's go through your packs to make sure you have everything you need and that you aren't taking anything unnecessary before we get on the bus."

"Umm, you have to go through our packs?" Avery asks, looking horrified.

"Yes." Maverick plants his fists on his hips. "Like it was stated in the email you received, you are allowed to bring anything you think you might want or need except drugs or alcohol."

"Okay," she agrees quietly.

"Let's go." Maverick moves first, and the rest of us follow.

When I get outside, I head for my Bronco to grab my pack from the trunk. As I start to pull it out, a hand lands on it, and I follow the arm that hand is attached to and find Tanner standing next to me.

"You don't need to drag it out. We can go through it here," he says as he starts to unzip the main zipper, making me panic.

"You can't go through my bag." I pull it from his grasp, and he tugs it back.

"Sunshine, I promise you I've seen it all, so there's nothing in your pack that's going to surprise me."

"That might be." I yank it back toward me. "But I have things in here that I don't want you to see."

"I get that, but I need to make sure you only have the necessities, because as your partner, if you can't carry your pack, I'm going to be the one lugging it around, and I'd rather not have to carry shit you can't or won't ever use."

"Fine." I let it go and stand back, crossing my arms over my chest, and he gives me a look that makes my stomach feel funny before he starts to pull everything out. "Do I get to go through your pack?" I ask, tapping my foot.

"If you want." His dimple pops out, and I quickly grab the waterproof bag with my bras and underwear in it before he can open it. "Have you tried walking around with this on your back since you packed it?"

"Yes."

"How did it feel?"

"Heavy," I admit as he stacks all my granola bars in a pile.

"It's going to feel heavier. After about twenty minutes of hiking, ten pounds will start to feel like a hundred." His eyes meet mine. "Do you need everything here?" He motions to the piles he's made.

"Probably not." I eye my granola bars, not sure I can bear to leave them.

"We got your meal request and know you're a vegetarian. We have food and snacks for you, so you won't go hungry. If I were you, I would leave the granola bars behind, along with the extra clothes and the camera."

"I can't leave my camera."

"Okay, bring the camera; leave everything else." He hands me my bag so I can start to repack it, and I leave out all the extra clothes I packed, and I keep one of the three books and a couple of my granola bars. "Don't judge me," I tell him as I shove them in one of the side pockets. "They're my favorite."

"In that case, I'll carry a couple of them in my pack for you, and the rest, I'll put in the kitchen inside the lodge. You don't want to come back to find your car's been broken into by a bear."

"Yeah, that would suck." I zip up my bag and then flip it around to my back. Once it's settled, I realize how much more comfortable it feels without the extra weight. Startling me, he grabs the clips hanging at my sides and pulls them around in front of me, hooking them together around my waist.

"How does that feel now?" He tightens the straps, and my breath lodges in my throat while my stomach dances.

"Good." I tip my head back, the energy between us seeming to take on a life of its own when our eyes meet.

"Good." His eyes drop to my mouth, and I lick my lips, watching his pupils dilate, then jump when a horn sounds. Clearing his throat, he steps back and grabs the rest of my granola bars before slamming my trunk. "You can go ahead and get on the bus."

"Thanks." I duck my head and rush away. As the bus drives us to our drop-off location, I try to figure out what the hell is going on with me and why Tanner is able to make me feel things I've never felt before.

Chapter 4

Tanner

Hearing Cybil laugh, I look to where she's standing with Jacob and Parker and curse under my breath. When I met her at the bar yesterday, I was stunned stupid by her beauty and wit and caught off guard by the instant attraction that bounced between us—or I hoped it was mutual. I didn't know I had just gone over her profile for the trip, which is something I do with every client because it gives me a chance to get to know them before I take them out on a retreat. I had no idea I would be spending the next week with her.

"Fuck, I'm so fucked," I grumble under my breath when I watch her bend over to retie her boots. I didn't think she could look more gorgeous than she did yesterday. But today, when she got out of her SUV dressed in hiking boots, slouchy socks, leggings, a white tee with a flannel tied around her waist, making her curves even more pronounced, I knew I was in trouble. She even had a handkerchief that matched her flannel tied around her head, her blonde hair in a messy bun.

Blake saw my reaction, too, judging by his constant cursing and the talk he gave me about fraternizing with clients when she went inside the lodge. A reminder I didn't need. I would never jeopardize my relationship with Blake or Maverick, the only family I've ever really had, and I sure as fuck wouldn't put our business at risk. That said, there has never been a woman to snag my attention the way Cybil has, so when this week is over, if this intense heat between us is still there, all bets are off. I just hope I can use this time to get to know her and keep my hands and my mouth to myself for the next six days and twelve hours.

"Everyone has their lunch, and Blake will be at the campsite around five with dinner," Maverick says as I sling my pack onto my back. "Are you good?"

"Yep."

"You're full of shit." He smirks, glancing over at Cybil.

"Don't you start with me too," I mutter and he laughs. Blake and Mav couldn't be more different. Ever since I met Blake on our first tour overseas, he's been a high-strung stickler for following the rules, while Mav has always just kinda gone with the flow and let the cards fall where they might. That's why the three of us have always worked so well together. I'm a little bit of both, depending on the circumstances.

"Just gonna say good luck with that." He pulls the satellite phone out of his back pocket, placing it in my open palm. "Call if you run into trouble."

"Will do." I lift my chin, then head over to the group.

"It's not common to see bears on the trail," Blake says as he hands a can of bear spray to each person. "But they are around, and so are cougars. Like we went over this morning, it's important for you to be aware of your surroundings and to watch out for your partner. Now, please do not use the bear spray unless there's a bear." He gives Lauren a look, and she quickly closes the safety latch. "Enjoy your hike, and I'll see you all tonight at the campsite for dinner." He walks past me, palming my shoulder. "They're all yours."

I walk to the front of the group and look to each person. "Jacob, Parker, you two are going to lead us up the trail, and Cybil and I will follow at the back of the group. Like Blake said, everyone needs to stay alert and aware, and if anyone needs a break, say something, and we'll all stop." I glance to everyone once more. "Make sure you're utilizing your hydration pack. You don't want to get dehydrated out here. Any questions?"

When no one speaks up, I motion for Jacob and Parker to take the lead, and as they head toward the trail cut into the side of the mountain, I hear the bus behind us start up.

"Have you ever run into a bear when you've been out here hiking?" Lauren asks me over her shoulder as Cybil falls into place at my side.

"A few times, but they typically take off when they hear us coming, so sightings are rare."

"At my house in Oregon, I ran into a black bear early one morning when I was going from my house to my shop, which is just across the driveway," Cybil says, then laughs. "I almost had a heart attack. Up until that point, I had only seen them from a distance, so I didn't know how big they really are up close."

"What happened?" Avery asks, glancing back at her.

"We stared at each other for what felt like forever; then he ran off, and I went back into my house to grab a pot and spoon so I could make some noise when I went back out." She laughs, and I chuckle. "I haven't seen him since that morning, but I know he's around, because every once in a while, my Ring camera will pick him up."

"How do you know it was a boy?" Lauren asks.

"I don't for sure, but when I googled how to tell the difference in case it was a mama with cubs, it said that male bears typically have larger, rounder faces, which makes it look like they have smaller ears."

"That's interesting," Avery says as she looks up at her husband. "Human males have big heads too."

"Witch." He chuckles, taking his wife's hand.

As the trail starts to take us up more of an incline, I scan the group to make sure everyone is doing okay. Before you can be approved for any retreat with Live Life Adventures, you're required to get a physical and fill out a questionnaire so we'll know exactly how hard we can push you. Cybil, Avery, and Lauren all stated in their information packets that they're active but not exactly adventurous in their activities, so I'll need to make sure the three of them are not pushing themselves too hard, too fast. One thing I learned from my time in the marines is it's easy to burn yourself out when you feel pressure from the people around you to perform above your ability.

"Have you always been a guide?" Cybil asks quietly, pulling me out of my thoughts, and I glance down at her, finding her watching her footing as we walk up the rocky path.

"No. Blake, Maverick, and I were in the marines. During our last tour overseas, we decided that when our time was up, we'd go into business together. And since we specialized in teamwork and survival skills in the military, we figured we'd transfer that knowledge to the real world."

"How long have you been out of the military?"

"I'll be out three years next month, and Mav and Blake got discharged a couple of months after I did."

"I'm sure you saw a lot overseas." She glances up at me, her eyes looking even bluer with the backdrop of the forests and the light coming in through the canopy of trees.

"We did," I agree but don't say more, and I'm thankful when she doesn't ask more questions. My time in the military isn't something I like to talk about, especially given some of the things I witnessed and experienced while overseas.

"So then you guys decided to move to Montana? Are you from here?"

"No, I grew up in Kentucky. Blake grew up here. His family lives in the valley, and his parents owned the land the lodge is on now. When we came to them with our business plan, they sold us ten acres of their property."

"That's cool. Where is Maverick from?"

"New Mexico."

"You and he are a long way from home. That must be hard for the two of you."

"Not as hard as you think," I say, and she looks up at me again, and I know she sees more than she should when her expression softens, making her even more beautiful. "What about you? Have you always lived in Oregon?"

"My whole life." She stumbles, but I catch her around her upper arm before she can fall. "Thanks," she breathes.

"Anytime." I let her go as we continue uphill, then realize where we are. "Jacob," I call out, and he stops to look at me as everyone else does the same. "We'll stop at the clearing about twenty minutes ahead and have lunch."

"Got it." He continues walking, and everyone follows suit.

When we reach the clearing, I use the sat phone to check in with Maverick, then go in search of Cybil when I don't see her with everyone else. Spotting her sitting on a log with a book in one hand and her sandwich in the other, I drop my pack and take my lunch with me to join her.

"What are you reading, sunshine?" I ask as I straddle the log, and she looks up at me midchew, then flips the cover closed so I can see for myself. I raise a brow when I see a medieval-looking couple kissing and the title *The King's Prize*. "Is it any good?"

Setting the book down, she picks up her water and takes a sip before answering. "I just started, but the author is one of my favorites, so I hope so."

"Hm." I pull out my sandwich and take a bite while she opens her book back up.

"You're staring at me," she says after a few minutes, and I chuckle, because there are not many women who say whatever it is they are thinking—at least not many that I've met.

"I like looking at you," I tell her honestly, watching her cheeks flush a pretty shade of pink.

"Well, stop," she mumbles without taking her eyes off her book. "It's making me feel weird."

"Weird," I repeat, and she turns toward me.

"Yes, weird, and shouldn't you be eating with everyone else?"

"Nope, mealtime is my time." I finish off the rest of my sandwich in one bite, and she sighs as she goes back to her book. "Why aren't *you* eating with everyone?"

"I'm used to being alone, so being around people for long periods of time drains my energy." Her eyes meet mine, and her nose scrunches. "Don't get me wrong—I like people; I just need quiet, if that makes sense."

"I'm the same way."

"Really?" She lifts a brow, and I smile.

"After a week out here with guests, I have to spend a couple of days alone. It drives Mav and Blake nuts when I go off the grid and they can't get ahold of me," I admit, wondering what else we might have in common because I haven't met many people who like to be alone.

"It makes my best friend, Jade, nuts too." She laughs, and fuck if the sound doesn't make my stomach muscles bunch. "Then again, she thinks I spend enough time alone, since I'm in my shop working on my own every day unless it's time to ship stuff out. Then I have my neighbor Earl there with me, helping box stuff up to be mailed out."

"What kind of shop do you have?"

"It's not a real shop. It's more like where I keep my materials and sewing machine. I design and sell vegan leather handbags at a few local stores and online through my website and social media."

"Really? How did you get into that?"

"My mom was a seamstress. She taught me how to sew, and when I became a vegetarian, I didn't feel good carrying a real leather bag. So I decided to make my own out of natural materials. The first time I wore one of my designs in town, a friend of mine saw it and wanted one, so

I made her one. Then I started getting calls, and the next thing I knew, my business was born." She shrugs.

"That's impressive—not many people have it in them to go after what they want or to build a business from the ground up."

"You did it," she says easily, and my chest feels funny. "It also doesn't hurt that it makes me happy and keeps a roof over my head." She stiffens ever so slightly when Lauren breaks away from everyone else and starts toward us.

"You okay?" I ask when she gets up and shoves her garbage into the reusable sack her lunch came in before tucking it and her book back into her pack.

"Yep, just gonna go take a few pictures." She pulls out her camera that is a lot more fancy than the ones people normally bring along on one of these trips and lifts the thick strap over her head so that it's hanging on her chest.

As I watch her go, I realize that even though she acted like what Lauren asked earlier didn't bother her, it obviously did, and I can't even blame her.

"Hey, Tanner." Lauren grabs my attention, and I lift my chin. "I was wondering about how far away the campsite is from here?"

"Without stopping, it's about a two-hour hike up the mountain, but I'd guess we'll make it there in three. Is everything okay?"

"Oh yeah." She takes a seat on the log, and I scoot back, uncomfortable about having her practically sitting on my lap. "Oliver needs to call his wife and kids to check in. Maverick told him that he could use the satellite phone when we get to camp."

"I'll make sure that he's able to make a call if he needs to."

"Thank you, Tanner." She leans toward me and lowers her voice. "He and his wife are going through a really ugly divorce, and I don't want her to have more to use against him when they go to court." She rests her hand on my biceps, and I somehow manage to keep my expression neutral.

"No problem." I stand as sourness fills the back of my throat: one thing I don't believe in is cheating, and I really hope that's not how their relationship started. "You should pack up. We're going to leave in a couple of minutes."

"Oh." She rubs her hands down the tops of her thighs, glancing to where Oliver is as she stands, her expression falling.

Not sure what that's about, I grab my pack and zip it up, then scan the area for Cybil, spotting her up the trail with her camera out, snapping photos of a squirrel that's sitting on a rock just off the path. "Let's load up and head out," I call to the rest of the group, who are standing around under a tree off the trail, and they all turn in my direction before grabbing their packs off the ground and moving toward Cybil.

"You're annoyed," Cybil whispers as she falls into step with me after everyone else passes, and my chin jerks back in surprise. No one but Blake and Maverick have ever been able to read me, and it took them years to be able to decipher my moods.

"Yeah," I agree, and she wraps her fingers around mine, squeezing quickly before letting her hand drop away.

"Well, turn that frown upside down." She knocks my shoulder playfully with her fist. "It's a beautiful day, the sun is shining, and we're on an adventure, partner."

Shaking my head, I smile down at her, feeling lighter than I did a minute ago. "All right, sunshine." I grin, watching her eyes go to the dimple in my cheek right before she ducks her head.

Fuck, but she's going to make it really difficult not to kiss her for the next week.

Chapter 5

Cybil

After picking up sticks and twigs I think will be good for firewood, I carry them to the pile that Parker, Jacob, and I have started, then go back in search of more. My body protests under its own weight as I walk with my eyes on the ground at my feet.

I'm exhausted. I thought I knew what exhaustion was before today, but after hiking uphill, carrying the weight of my pack, I now know I was wrong. I also hope Tanner is right that, as the days pass, it will get easier.

"So Tanner's cute," Jacob says casually as he walks past me with his arms full, and my heart skips a beat at the mention of the man I spent the day getting to know.

"Very cute," Parker chimes in. "Don't you think so, Cybil?"

"Sure." I drop my eyes to the ground and start to walk away, knowing where their line of questioning is going.

"He seems to like you."

Does he? I bite my bottom lip. "It's his job to be nice to me." I don't know if that's true, but I do know the feelings he stirs in me are ones I've never experienced before.

"Honey, that man is smitten," Jacob says, and I focus on him.

"Can't you tell?" Parker asks with his head tipping to the side as he studies me, and I shrug. "How did you know your ex liked you?"

"We were friends, so I always knew." And that's the truth. Galvin and I grew up together. He, Jade, and I weren't just close; we were inseparable. It wasn't until I was about to be sixteen that things between Galvin and me started to change and become more flirtatious. It's weird to think about it now, but it seemed natural for our relationship to progress.

"Wait." Jacob frowns. "How long were you together?"

"A little over nine years."

"Jesus, you were just a baby," he whispers, sounding horrified.

"We were both sixteen," I say in my defense.

"And he's the only man you've ever been with?" Parker asks, and my cheeks warm as I nod. "Why did things end between the two of you?"

"Don't answer that." Jacob glares at his husband.

"I couldn't even if I wanted to," I tell them quietly. "He didn't tell me why he didn't want to be with me anymore. He just kept saying it was him, not me."

"Obviously, he didn't lie. You're gorgeous, funny, and—"

"And you don't know me well," I tell Parker as I laugh. "It's okay." I wave my hand out. "You don't have to try to make me feel better. Just please don't start feeling sorry for me."

"I . . . ," Parker starts, but whatever he was about to say is cut off when we hear what sounds like a four-wheeler coming through the trees.

"That's probably Blake," Jacob says, looking between Parker and me. "We should finish up and get back to camp—I don't know about you two, but I'm starving and ready to go to sleep."

Without another word, the three of us split up to finish our task. Once we're done and are loaded up with firewood, we make our way back to camp, where the rest of the group has been clearing the area and digging a pit for the fire. With my arms full, I clear the trees and automatically search out Tanner, finding him standing next to Blake, the two of them talking quietly. Like he senses me watching him, he turns his head my way, and our eyes lock for a moment before I duck my head and drop my armful of branches onto the pile Jacob and Parker started.

"Everyone, come here and gather around," Tanner calls out, and everyone stops what they're doing and heads toward where he's still standing with Blake next to a four-wheeler that is loaded down with coolers and canvas bags. "Each couple is responsible for setting up their tent when we reach camp each evening and taking it down each morning after breakfast," he says as Blake passes out canvas bags to each couple. "In the pamphlet you were given this morning were instructions on how to go about setting up your tent. You must follow them and work with your partner to complete the task at hand, and if you don't, both of you will be sleeping outside in the elements for the night."

His eyes meet mine when Blake hands me a tent, and it's not until that moment that I realize I'll be sharing a tent with Tanner.

Holy cow.

"Let's get this done so we can eat," he says, releasing me from his gaze, and I gulp as I numbly carry the canvas bag across the dirt area. I drop it to the ground, then grab my pack and dig out the papers I was given this morning.

"It's really unfair that she has Tanner helping her," I hear Lauren complain, and I grit my teeth to keep from saying something to her I might regret. I've never disliked anyone, not really anyway, but there's something about her that rubs me the wrong way and sets me on edge.

"Ignore her," Tanner says quietly, squatting down next to me, and I sigh as I read over the directions, wanting to have a basic idea of what needs to be done before I start the task and work through the steps. When I finish, I set the paper aside and remove the tent and poles from the bag, then start to unfold it and lay it flat with Tanner's help.

"We need something to get the stakes into the ground," I tell him, getting up and looking around for a rock. When I finally find one, he takes it from me and pounds the four posts into the ground with ease, then waits patiently for me to tell him what we have to do next. Even though I'm sure he's done this a million times, the small gesture makes me feel essential to the process. With the next step being to set up all the poles, I do that; then we work together to weave them through the canvas loops before we raise the roof.

Once we're finished, I can't help my smile, feeling proud of myself. Not only did I keep up with the group today but I just helped set up our shelter for the night. I look around and find that everyone else is finishing up as well. I grab my bag and duck my head as I take the bag into the tent, then I take a seat on the floor and lie down, wanting to close my eyes for just a few minutes. "I'm so tired," I admit when I feel him take a seat near me.

"You did great today."

"All I did was walk." My lips twitch into a smile when he chuckles.

"Yeah, but you didn't spend the entire time complaining, and like I said, every day, it will get a little easier."

"I hope so." I yawn, covering my mouth.

"Come on. Since you finished first, you can help me start the fire."

"Shouldn't the winner get a chance to rest?" I joke, opening my eyes to find him standing over me.

"Nope." He holds out his hand, so I take it, and he helps pull me up off the ground, which is good, since I'm not sure I would have been able to get up on my own. "You can rest after you put some food in your stomach."

"Fine, but only because I'm starving and wouldn't be able to sleep with my stomach growling anyway," I say, and he laughs as I follow him out of the tent.

After we get the fire started, he and Blake bring over a large metal-looking swing with a horizontal floating sheet pan that they place over the fire. Then, the two of them set about getting dinner ready while the rest of the group sits around and talks.

With the evening getting cooler, I'm untying my flannel from my waist and putting it on when Avery comes over to join me on the log I'm sitting on.

"Are you doing okay?" she asks, tucking her hands into the sleeves of her sweatshirt.

"Yeah, just tired. Are you doing all right?"

"I just wish I could shower." She grimaces. "Of everything I thought of when I agreed to take this trip with Grant, it never once crossed my mind that I wouldn't be able to shower for a week."

"I didn't think about that either." I tuck my hands between my thighs to warm up my fingers.

"At least we'll *all* stink."

"True." I laugh, and she giggles, then her back straightens and her eyes narrow across the fire. Lauren has taken a seat right next to Avery's husband and starts talking to him with a flirtatious smile.

"That girl," she mumbles, shaking her head. "Oliver seems so nice; I don't know what he's doing with her."

"I don't either," I agree, spotting Oliver sitting with Parker and Jacob, playing a game with a deck of cards and not paying attention to Lauren. Then again, maybe that's her problem; maybe she's trying to find a way to get his attention. "Maybe we just don't know her."

"I've known women like her my whole life. They are never happy unless every man in their orbit is circling around them." She turns to face me. "She's barking up the wrong tree with Grant, and judging by the way Tanner reacted to her touching him earlier, he's cut from the same cloth."

She touched Tanner? My stomach twists at the thought.

"Some men get off on women being aggressive, but then there are those who like to do the chasing. My husband is the latter, and I'm guessing Tanner is the same way."

Unsure what to say to that, I don't say anything. Jade always said how lucky I was not to be out in the dating pool, and now I know she was probably right, because it all seems like a very confusing game of cat and mouse that I don't know how to play.

"Who's ready to eat?" Blake calls out, and on cue, my stomach rumbles.

As we eat, the conversation is light, mostly centering around tomorrow. We're scheduled to hike down the mountain, where Maverick will meet us with a raft that we'll take downriver to where we're going to have lunch. As I eat, I'm happily surprised with my meal of vegetable shish kebabs, bean soup, and buttered rolls, and everyone else seems just as pleased with their meat options.

When we finish, we help Blake load up the dishes before he takes off on the four-wheeler, leaving all of us to enjoy s'mores and warm cider or cocoa before getting ready for bed. Which isn't much fun, since it includes using the bathroom in the middle of the woods—something I'm not sure I'll ever get used to.

After I brush my teeth and change into a pair of sleep pants and a long-sleeved top, I climb into my sleeping bag and chew the inside of my cheek as I listen to Tanner talk to Parker and Jacob. I know logically that I shouldn't be nervous about sleeping in the same space as him, especially since we have separate sleeping bags and enough space between us for another two people. But I feel anxious and on edge as I wait for him to come to bed. After tossing and turning a dozen times, I grab my book and headlamp from my bag, hoping that reading will take my mind off everything and relax me enough that I'll be able to fall asleep.

Feeling my head being lifted, I blink my eyes open, then hold my breath when I find Tanner leaning over me. "Hey," he says quietly as he takes my book from my grasp. "You fell asleep. I didn't think you'd want to sleep with your headlamp on all night."

"Thanks." My voice sounds sleepy, and I catch his grin right before he turns the light off, and I hear the sound of it hitting the ground at my hip.

"So did the king get his prize?" he asks, and I hear the smile in his voice right before a thud, then another, that I'm guessing are his boots hitting the ground.

"Not yet. Katharine is being difficult."

"Women." He chuckles, and my breath catches as I hear the whoosh of clothing and then the sound of a zipper.

Oh my goodness, he's getting undressed.

"Maybe it's him," I say, needing to fill the silence as I squeeze my eyes closed, which is ridiculous, because it's completely dark. "He can't just expect her to be okay after he came into her life and flipped it upside down."

"Maybe she needs to trust him."

"Well, Mr. Couples Retreat Expert, haven't you been preaching all day long that trust is *earned*?"

I hear him still completely and wait for him to reply like I'm waiting for my next breath.

"You're right, sunshine," he says quietly as I hear him get into his sleeping bag. "Trust *is* earned. But sometimes, you need to be open to trusting someone else in order for things to work."

"True." I roll to my side, placing my back to him, then add softly, "Hopefully, she can do that, because she deserves to be happy." I close my eyes while scooting down deeper into my sleeping bag and wrapping my arms around my middle. "Night, Tanner."

"Night, sunshine," he says gruffly, and I swallow over the lump that has suddenly formed in my throat.

As I lie there in the dark, listening to the sound of his breathing even out, I wonder if he feels even a little of what I do . . . and what it all means. Galvin never made me feel the way Tanner does, and we were together for years. I want to say I was in love with him, but did I love him more as a friend? Was I going to marry him because it was kind of always the plan? With those thoughts rolling around in my head, it takes me forever to find sleep, even though I'm exhausted.

Chapter 6

CYBIL

I slowly start to wake when the light of the rising sun begins to beat against my closed eyelids, and I shiver when the chilly morning air brushes against my face. Seeking out the warmth of my sleeping bag, I try to burrow into it, but my legs and waist are stuck under a heavy solid object. I start to force myself free, then freeze when I hear a grunt, and my heart starts to pound.

Tanner.

Without even opening my eyes, I know it's him who has me trapped. I roll in my sleeping bag in an attempt to get away, not sure how I got across the space between us in the first place, then stop suddenly when I run into the canvas wall of the tent, causing it to shake. Stilling completely, I hold my breath and wait to see if I hear any sign that I've woken him up, but nothing but the sound of birds chirping and his steady breaths greets my ears.

Peeking my head out of my sleeping bag, I look across the brightly lit space and see him lying on his side, his eyes closed, and his chest rising and falling rhythmically. I carefully roll to my stomach, trying not to make any noise, and every muscle in my body protests as I crawl out of my sleeping bag. Once I'm free, I crawl my way to the opening and just as quietly unzip the tent before I head into the woods to take care of business. When I make it back to camp, Oliver is coming out of his and Lauren's tent, looking just as sleepy as I feel.

"Morning, Oliver." I give him a small wave.

"Good morning, Cybil. Did you sleep okay?"

"Yes, did you?"

"I've slept better." He stretches his arms over his head. "See you in a bit." He heads to the woods, and I dive back into my tent, zipping it closed.

Crawling on my hands and knees toward my sleeping bag with dreams of snoozing for a little while longer, I become paralyzed when Tanner's gruff "Morning, sunshine" stops me in my tracks. I swing my head in his direction. "Did you sleep okay?" The question is innocent enough, but there's a knowing glint in his eyes that causes heat to rise up my neck to my cheeks.

"Um, great. D-did you?" I stutter out.

"Better than I normally do." He sits up, and I swallow when I see he doesn't have a shirt on, which means I'm able to see exactly how perfect he is. My eyes roam over his thick arms, landing on his broad chest that has a scattering of dark hair between his pecs and then traveling down the middle of his abs—and I'm sure farther, but I can't see past the sleeping bag that's gathered around his waist. "Cybil?"

Licking my lips, I meet his gaze, and my stomach flutters when I see his smirk. "Yeah?"

"I asked if you're hungry?"

Oh my God, I didn't hear him ask me anything. I didn't even hear him speak until he said my name. "Yes, sorry, I think I'm still half-asleep," I lie, and he grins as he unzips his bag and then stands. I quickly scramble up on my knees and tip my head back to keep my eyes on his so I don't get caught checking him out again—something that is really hard not to do.

"It's still early." He bends to grab his shirt, then gathers it up before pulling it over his head. "I'm going to start coffee." He glances at his watch, then drops his eyes back to mine. "Blake will be here in about twenty minutes with breakfast. The tent is all yours until then."

"Thanks." I glance longingly at my sleeping bag, wanting nothing more than to crawl back into it and sleep for the rest of the day, or maybe even the rest of the week.

"You can go to sleep early tonight," he tells me softly, and I glance at him before I fall to my bottom and pull my pack toward me. "When you're ready, we'll take down the tent."

"Okay, thanks," I mutter to my lap as I search for the package of wet wipes I brought with me, just so I can do something to keep from staring at him like I want to. When the zipper sounds, I lift my head and watch him step outside, then fall to my back and stare at the top of the tent. I have no idea how the hell I'm going to survive the next few days without doing something stupid, like asking him to kiss me.

With my heart seeming to want to escape my chest, I watch everyone as they climb into the raft that will take us downriver. I originally wasn't nervous about this part of the trip, because I knew the rapids weren't going to be rough, but after listening to Maverick and Tanner go over all the instructions—*and there were a lot of them*—I don't know if I'm ready for this. And worse, I'm Tanner's partner, so I've been placed in charge of helping him, which seems a whole lot ridiculous, since I have no idea what I'm doing. I've never even been in a boat before.

"Sunshine, you doing okay?" Tanner asks, coming to stand at my side, and I peek up at him and shake my head. "What's wrong?"

"I'm afraid that I'm going to mess up and send everyone into the water," I admit, and he chuckles. "It's not funny." I narrow my eyes on his.

"It won't happen, Cybil. The water is going to be calm the entire way downstream. You have nothing to worry about." He takes my hand,

and I jolt at the contact. "Easy, sweetheart. I promise I got you," he says quietly. "I'll be with you the entire time."

"Have you ever had a boat tip over?" I ask, refusing to budge from my spot on the bank.

"Rafting in class-six rapids, yes, but this area of the river we're going down is a class one at best." He gives my fingers a squeeze, then releases my hand and turns me to face him, quickly making sure that all the buckles on my life jacket are where they should be and tightening the ones that are loose. When he's finished, he locks his gaze with mine and touches the end of my nose with his fingertip. "I promise I won't let anything happen to you." He takes my hand and helps me into the raft. Once I'm settled on my seat, he takes his place next to me and hands me my paddle, and I copy the hold he has on his.

"Ready?" Maverick asks, and everyone yells in the affirmative while my hands tremble. "See you at the bottom." He wades out into the river, pushing the raft out to send us on our way.

As we slowly float downstream, with Tanner giving us instructions on what we should do with our paddles, my heartbeat starts to return to normal, and I begin to relax enough to lift the camera hanging around my neck and snap a few photos. It's beautiful out here, and with tall tree-covered mountains on each side of the river and the bright-blue sky above us, a sense of peace settles over me. Like everything that has happened to bring me to this moment doesn't really matter.

"Are you doing okay, sunshine?" Tanner asks quietly, and I turn to focus on his handsome face, which looks even better with the thick stubble covering his cheeks.

"Yeah." I drag in a breath of fresh air, and his expression gentles.

"Good." He reaches over to give my thigh a squeeze, which causes tingles to shoot through my system like little fireworks. When he turns around to check on everyone, I focus on the water ahead as memories of all the times Galvin touched me just like that roll through my mind.

I have no feelings of loss or sadness connected to those memories, but there is a whole lot of confusion.

Being with Galvin was easy. He was my friend. Like Jade, I could tell him anything, talk to him about everything, and just be with him without pressure. It's odd to realize now that the one thing missing in our relationship was chemistry. He didn't cause my pulse to race with a simple touch and he didn't make my stomach dance when he looked at me, and because it was something I never had, I never knew I was missing it.

Chewing the inside of my cheek, I wonder if that's why he ended things. I wonder if he found that with someone else and realized he wanted more. If that's what happened, I can't fault him, because now that Tanner has brought these feelings out in me, I know what I was missing. I also wonder if I would feel the same with anyone else or if this is just a result of the connection I feel to the man at my side.

"Oh my God, there's a bear!" Lauren shouts, bringing me out of my thoughts, and I scan the shoreline until my eyes land on the huge brown bear near the edge of the river.

"That's a grizzly." I hear the confusion in Tanner's voice. "What's he doing here?"

"What do you mean?" I ask as I study the bear sweeping his paw through the water.

"They aren't common in this area."

"They aren't?" I turn to look at him, and he shakes his head.

"I've heard there've been sightings, but I thought they were just rumors."

"Apparently, they aren't." I turn back just in time to watch the large bear stand on his hind legs and lift his snout in our direction, making a huffing sound. "He's huge." I swallow, intimidated and awed by his size. He's much bigger than the black bear I saw at my house in Oregon, probably three times bigger. "I hope I never run into him."

"You and me both," Parker says, and the rest of the boat breaks into quiet murmurs of agreement.

"I doubt we'll see him again; we're going to be a ways away from here," Tanner says, looking at me. "Take a couple photos of him for me, sunshine."

"Sure," I agree, realizing that I was so caught up in the moment I didn't even think about my camera. As we drift past the bear that's now back to pawing at the water, probably searching for fish to eat, I snap a few pictures.

"When we reach shore, I'll pass your camera off to Maverick so he can stop at the ranger station and let them know there's a grizzly in the area. Hopefully, they'll be able to use the pictures to narrow down the location and put out an alert for people who might be hiking," he says, looking over my shoulder at the screen on my camera as I slide through the photos.

"So Cybil is going to have to give up her camera?" Oliver asks, sounding annoyed on my behalf. "For how long?"

"It's fine. I don't mind." I wave off his concern.

"But it's your camera, Cybil. You're always taking pictures and—"

"She said she doesn't mind, Oli. Just let it go," Lauren snaps, cutting him off, and I sigh as the two of them start to bicker, something they've been doing since breakfast, when Lauren found out she couldn't get some fancy coffee creamer she always uses.

When Tanner rests his hand on my thigh and squeezes to get my attention, I turn to focus on him. "I'll make sure Mav knows to give your camera to Blake so he can bring it back to you when he drives up dinner tonight."

"It's really not a big deal," I groan.

"Hush, we don't want to upset Oli." He winks, and I drop my eyes to his mouth, catching his grin before he returns his focus to passing out orders. With a smile, I place my paddle back into the water and help him get us downriver, and I have to admit—we make a darn good team.

Chapter 7

TANNER

"All right, come gather around," I call out when I hear Blake coming up the mountain on his four-wheeler, and everyone stops what they're doing to join me. "I have some good news and some bad news. Once Blake gets here, we'll pass out tents just like yesterday, but unlike yesterday, you will not be allowed to use the instructions that were given to you in your pamphlet. You'll have to work together with your partner to set your tent up. The good news is, you get to leave it up in the morning, since we'll be camping in this location for two nights."

"What do you mean we can't use the instructions to set up our tents?" Lauren asks as Blake pulls up and parks behind me. Looking at her, I'm not surprised she's the only one with a sour look on her face.

"It's fine, Lauren. We'll figure it out," Oliver says, trying to assure her.

"Do you remember the steps to set up the tent?" She turns to face him, placing her hands on her hips. "Because I do not, and I have no desire to sleep outside."

"We're not going to be sleeping outside," he says, sounding exasperated.

"I'm just saying this isn't fair." She tosses her arms in the air. "Especially when Cybil gets to have Tanner's help, and the rest of us have to just figure it out."

"Then Tanner won't help me," Cybil says, and I look to where she's standing and find her with her arms wrapped around her middle.

"Cybil." My jaw starts to tic as she shakes her head.

"You won't help me." Anger wars with pride when I see the determination in her gaze. I have no doubt she'll be able to set the tent up on her own, but she shouldn't have to. I also have a gut feeling that if I try to step in right now, she won't be happy.

"Good," Lauren snaps.

"That's ridiculous." Jacob glares at Lauren.

"I'll help you," Avery says, and Cybil shakes her head.

"I appreciate that, Avery, but this is not the first time Lauren has implied that I'm getting off easy because I have Tanner as my partner, so hopefully after I do this, she'll stop bringing it up."

"Cybil, you don't have to do that," Oliver says quietly.

"It's fine." She moves to where Blake is now standing at my side, watching what's going down. "Can I please get a tent so I can get this over with?"

"Sure, babe." He unties one from the back, and once he hands it to her, he adds, "I also got your camera back from Mav." He hands that to her as well, and with a lift of her chin, she takes both and stomps off.

"You're unbelievable," Parker hisses to Lauren before he takes a tent from Blake and walks off with Jacob following, and Lauren turns to watch them go. Then she grabs her own tent and Oliver's hand to drag him off.

"I really do not like that girl." Avery sighs, and Grant shakes his head.

"Leave it, baby."

"I am leaving it, Grant, but that doesn't mean I can't say I don't like her."

"Right." He presses his lips together like he's trying not to laugh, and she narrows her eyes on him.

"You'd better not even think about laughing right now."

"Baby, I see you're itching for an argument, but how about you put all that energy you have into helping me set up our tent?" he suggests.

"How about you sleep outside tonight?" she hisses before stomping past Blake to grab her own tent from the back of the four-wheeler and carrying it away.

"So I'm just gonna put this out there. Maybe you two wanna rethink adding this kind of situation into your future retreats," Grant says, looking between Blake and me before turning on his heel and following after his wife.

"So I see Lauren is still adding her special brand of joy to every occasion," Blake mutters from my side.

"The woman doesn't know when to stop," I grumble back.

"Well, something tells me that Oliver isn't going to care how pretty she is, if she isn't careful," he says. Then he adds, "Damn, Cybil's got a lot of pent-up anger."

I follow his gaze to where Cybil is and curse under my breath when I see her using a large rock to pound the poles into the ground with a little too much force. "You're gonna have to replace those stakes tomorrow."

"Yeah." He sighs. "Let's get dinner on. Hopefully some food will cheer everyone up."

For the next hour, I help him get dinner ready over the fire as each couple works on setting up their tent, and I'm proud as fuck to see Cybil is keeping up with everyone else, even on her own. When she finishes, all the other couples have already gathered around the fire and are starting to eat.

I want to pull her into my arms when she walks over to join us, and it pisses me off that I can't.

"I'm not sure our tent will make it through the night, partner," she tells me quietly as she takes the bowl I hold out to her.

"That's okay. I prefer sleeping under the stars anyway." At my statement, her eyes drift up to meet mine. "I'm fucking proud of you, sunshine."

"Thank you." She drops her gaze to my mouth, and my fingers clench into fists. Every fucking time she does that, it takes all my willpower not to tangle my hand in her hair, tip her head back, and kiss her like I know she wants—like both of us want.

"You need to eat," I order softly, and she rubs her lips together before nodding and taking a seat on the log behind us. Sitting next to her, I dig into my bowl of stew, while she eats some broccoli cheddar soup that smelled delicious as I was heating it up. When we both finish, I take our bowls and dump them in the cooler on the back of the four-wheeler, then grab a plate of chicken and corn for myself and the single-size pizza loaded with roasted vegetables for her.

"I don't know who your guys' chef is, but I want to take them home with me," she tells me after she finishes off half her pizza.

"That would be Blake's mom, Janet." I smile as she rubs her stomach. "When we started running guided trips, she told us that if we wanted to be successful, we needed to offer five-star meals for clients to enjoy at the end of each day. We thought she didn't know what she was talking about, but we've had a lot of people come back just because of the food."

"That doesn't surprise me. The meals would be one of the reasons I would want to come back."

"What are the other reasons?" I ask curiously.

"Honestly, everything. I didn't think I would enjoy this trip, but it's actually been fun trying new things and pushing myself. Plus, you're not so bad to hang out with."

"Good to know." I chuckle, and she bounces her shoulder off mine. "Are you done eating?" I ask, eyeing what's left of her pizza, and she laughs.

"You want my leftovers, don't you?"

"I've always been a guy who enjoys meat, but every time you get your food, all I can think is I'm missing out."

"You are. Vegetables are delicious." She passes me her plate, and I take a large bite and groan in approval. "Told you so."

"What made you become a vegetarian?" I ask, knowing she implied she didn't always avoid eating meat as I take another bite.

Her eyes wander from mine, and she takes a deep breath. "My mom got cancer and wanted to do everything right, so she started eating a strict vegan diet. I wasn't as disciplined as her, but I never loved meat, so I just stopped eating it. Which made it easier when she was cooking. I guess it just kind of stuck."

"Is your mom okay now?" I ask softly, and she shakes her head.

"She passed away when I was fifteen. She fought for six years before she couldn't fight anymore."

"Jesus, Cybil." I wrap my arms around her shoulders when I see her eyes start to water, and she burrows her face in my chest. "I'm so fucking sorry, baby."

"It's okay. I'm okay." She sniffles and pulls away, wiping her cheeks. "I don't know why I'm crying right now. I think I'm just really tired."

I'm sure she is tired, but as she avoids looking at me, I wonder if she's really dealt with the loss of her mom or if she's tucked the pain away and built up walls around it to keep from facing what she went through. From experience, I know it seems easier to evade the past when it's painful, but fuck if those doors you think are locked don't have a way of opening up when you least expect.

"You should go try to sleep."

"Yeah." She stands and glances through me. "I'll see you in the morning."

"Night, sunshine," I say quietly, watching her say good night to everyone else before she heads for our tent. After I watch her disappear,

I get up and take our plates to the back of the four-wheeler, then help Blake load up and send him on his way.

After making sure that camp is secure and the campfire is out, I lie in my sleeping bag and listen to Cybil breathe. Just as I'm beginning to drift off, she rolls in her sleeping bag toward me and presses into my side, just like she did last night. For a long moment, I don't move, not even taking a breath.

I should wake her up. I know I should put distance between us, but just like last night, I wait until I know she won't wake up, then curl around her. I fall asleep, enjoying every fucking second of having her close.

Chapter 8

Cybil

"Cybil."

When I hear my name, my eyes flutter open, and I frown when I see Tanner leaning over me, fully dressed and wearing a headlamp similar to the one I have.

"Is everything okay?" I look around, noticing it's still mostly dark, the beige tent letting through just a glimmer of early-morning light.

"Yeah, I have something to show you. Get dressed and meet me outside."

"Are you going to take me into the woods to murder me before everyone else wakes up?"

"No." He grins. "Come on. You gotta hurry up, and don't forget your camera and headlamp."

"Okay," I agree as curiosity and excitement make my pulse quicken. I unzip my bag and climb out as he leaves the tent. It takes me less than five minutes to get dressed in a pair of leggings, a long sweater with my vest over it, boots, and my knit cap. When I get outside, I find Tanner waiting for me with a thermos in one hand.

"Come on, sunshine," he whispers again, holding out his hand for me to take, and the moment our palms connect, a tingle travels down my spine and my stomach flutters.

"Where are we going?" I ask quietly as we walk through the woods with the canopy of trees above us, making it seem darker than it is.

"You'll see when we get there." He gives my fingers a squeeze, and we walk in comfortable silence until I notice that the trees off in the distance open up. As we get closer, I hear the sound of running water and can see the yellow sky above the range. "I found this place during the first trip I guided, and since then, I've been back at least a dozen times," he says quietly as we step out of the trees and onto the bank of a rocky shore at the bottom of a small waterfall that is shooting out the side of the mountain. "I thought you'd like to get some pictures."

I hold my breath as I take in the beauty all around me, then tip my head back. The sun is coming up, and the stars are fighting to keep their place in the sky for just a little while longer, creating a picture that feels ethereal.

"This is beautiful."

"It is," Tanner says softly, and I turn to find him watching me. When I shiver, not from cold but from the look in his eyes, he holds out the thermos he's been carrying. "I got us some cocoa, but we'll have to share the cup."

I nod and walk to where he is, then take a seat next to him on a large log that's been half hollowed out.

"Thank you for bringing me here." I take the mug of cocoa from his grasp when he hands it to me and blow across the hot liquid, watching steam disappear into the cool morning air. "I've seen lots of pictures of places just like this, pictures that I thought were photoshopped. It's unbelievable to me that I'm sitting here in the middle of perfection and I know that it's real."

"Have you traveled a lot?"

"No, I . . . I think I've gotten a little too comfortable in my safe little bubble. But after this trip I want to change that."

"There's lots of life to experience."

"I'm realizing that," I say; then he leans in close to me.

"Don't make a sound or any sudden movement," he whispers, and my heart stops before it starts to pound as I imagine the grizzly from yesterday walking toward us. "Look to your left, downstream about fifty feet."

I slowly turn my head, and that's when I spot a group of elk working their way across the water, with the male in front sporting a huge set of antlers.

"Hold this, please." I hand him the cup so I can lift my camera. As I power it on, the noise it makes seems louder than normal, and the elk all freeze and look in our direction.

"Hurry, they're gonna run," Tanner warns with a smile in his voice, so I quickly lift my camera and hold down the shutter button as they begin to take off into the woods.

When they all disappear, I slide through the photos I just took and pout when I find that all but a couple are just a blur of movement. "I need a quieter camera."

"Let me see."

I hand it over and watch him go into my settings to change all of them to silent before he slides through the pictures, reaching the final one of the elk and pressing the button again, which causes the reel to return to the first picture I ever took with my camera. It's one of my ex with a goofy smile on his boyishly handsome face. Stiffening, I fight the urge to snatch my camera from Tanner's grasp and toss it into the water, not because seeing Galvin is upsetting but because I don't want Tanner and my not-so-distant past to meet.

"Your ex?"

"Yeah" is all I can seem to get out as his silence makes me squirm.

"What happened between you two?" he asks, handing my camera to me, and I quickly turn it off and let it fall back against my chest.

"I'm not sure." I take the hot cocoa back and take a sip as I look out at the landscape, and I'm thankful for his silence as I pull up the courage to tell him the truth. "Like any couple, we had our share of problems; we broke up a few times but always got back together . . ." I let out a breath. "I knew when he told me that he wanted to end things this time that it was for good, even though he didn't give me a reason."

"He didn't tell you why he was ending things?"

"No, he just kept saying it wasn't me; it was him. Since I've been here, I've started to wonder if he didn't find someone else who made him happy."

"Cybil."

Without looking at him, I shake my head. "We've known each other since we were five. He and Jade were always my best friends. Before we were even teenagers, all everyone ever talked about was how he and I would end up together, so when it happened, I thought everyone was right. Now, I don't think they were."

"What do you mean?" he asks, and I look over at him, swallowing hard.

"Have you ever met someone who made your pulse race to the point of lightheadedness, or someone who made you feel like you were coming out of your skin with one look?"

"Yeah," he says with his eyes locked on mine, and jealousy makes my skin prickle as I wonder how many women have given him that feeling.

"I never felt that until recently. I . . . I didn't even know those feelings even existed before now." I grip the cup in my hand tighter as his eyes seem to darken and his jaw twitches.

"Who made you feel those things?" he asks roughly, and I rub my lips together.

"You," I admit, sure that I should keep that information to myself.

"Come here, Cybil," he orders, but he doesn't actually give me a chance to come to him. His hand shoots out, and his fingers wrap around the base of my scalp; then he angles my head just like he wants it and drops his mouth to mine.

The first brush of his lips makes me dizzy; then his tongue slides across my bottom lip, causing my nipples to tighten and the space between my legs to pulse. My mouth falls open on a gasp, and he takes the opportunity to tangle his tongue with mine. As the kiss deepens, I despise the mug in my hands, because all I want to do is touch him back, to run my fingers through his thick hair and dig my nails into his skin.

"Jesus, Cybil," he groans, resting his forehead against mine, and I whimper in agreement, not sure I'll be able to take much more, not without dropping hot cocoa all over us.

I moan when he leans in to nip my bottom lip and whimper as he places a soft kiss and a swipe of his tongue against my abused mouth. "Wow." My eyes flutter open, and I find him watching me like I'm the most fascinating thing he's ever seen in his life, when I know that's far from the truth, given the life he's lived.

"Are you okay?"

Am I okay? I'm not sure. I feel like I've stepped into a raging river while attached to a live wire, and all my nerve endings are standing at attention like they're waiting to see what will happen next.

"I've wanted to do that since you told me off at the bar." He smirks at the memory as he smooths the tips of his fingers over my cheek. "And a dozen times since then." His eyes focus on his fingers as they tuck my hair behind my ear.

"Really?" I ask, and he tips his head down until his gaze locks with mine. When I see the look he gives me, my pulse that had slowed speeds right back up.

"You've tested my control these last few days, sunshine."

"Oh." I lick my lips, liking that he wants me as much as I want him, that I'm not the only one who's been fighting all these feelings. "I've wanted to kiss you too." I smile while adding, "Though when we first met, I really wanted to kick you."

Laughing, he leans back, taking the mug of cocoa from my grasp. "I guessed that when you brushed me off."

"You deserved it."

"Yeah," he says softly, putting the lid on the thermos and wrapping his arm around my shoulders to pull me into his side. I lean into him with a smile on my face, then jump a mile when a loud bang echoes through the quiet morning air, causing the birds in the nearby trees to take flight.

"What was that?" I ask as he bolts to his feet and looks around.

"Gunshot. My guess, a twelve gauge." He spins in a full circle, scanning the tree line before facing me. "Come on." He reaches for my hand, and as he pulls me up off the log, there's another shot, this one sounding closer. "Let's get back to camp."

Without another word, he tucks me into his side and leads me quickly back through the forest. As soon as we make it to camp, we find that everyone is up and standing outside their tents, looking sleepy but concerned.

"Where have you two been?" Lauren asks accusingly when she spots us, and I force Tanner to release my hand, wanting badly to tell her it's none of her business. But I know this is his job, and I don't want to jeopardize his or his friends' reputation.

"There were gunshots," Parker says, sending a scolding look in Lauren's direction before he looks between Tanner and me. "One of them was really close."

"We heard them too," I tell him.

"What's in season in terms of hunting?" Oliver asks, looking around.

"Nothing," Tanner tells him while dipping into the tent and coming out a moment later with the satellite phone.

As he walks off, putting the phone to his ear, I scan the area. I'm sure the sound of gunshots is normal in the mountains, but that doesn't put me at ease. All it would take is someone shooting in our direction, not knowing we are here, to seriously injure one of us.

"I'd still like to know what you were doing in the woods with Tanner," Lauren says, and I inwardly groan. I knew her giving up on Tanner and me was too much to ask for.

"You know, Lauren, I'm starting to think you have a thing for Tanner," Oliver says, and her expression hardens.

"Well, it seems to me that you have a thing for Cybil," she snaps. "You're always looking at her and standing up for her."

"Here we go again," he says, cutting her off. "Like I've told you before, it's called being a good person. I'm not interested in Cybil." Then he turns his back on her and slips inside their tent, with her quickly diving in after him. The two of them start to argue like they're in a room with four walls rather than a fabric tent. I look around and see Jacob and Parker both staring at Oliver and Lauren's tent with wide eyes as they shout about me, while Grant is nudging Avery, attempting to get her to look away.

"Maverick is going to ride up with Blake," Tanner says as he steps out of the woods. "Since we're staying here tonight, they're going to do a sweep of the area to see if they can find who fired the shots and let them know people are camping here. But since we haven't heard another shot, my guess is they already left the area."

"Have you heard shots fired out here before when you've been on a guided trip?" I ask, wrapping my arms around my waist, and his gaze comes to me, his jaw hardening as he takes me in.

"It's not abnormal . . ." His words trail off when Lauren emerges from the tent and screams at him.

"Tanner, I want to go home!"

"Lauren." Oliver scampers out behind her. "If you leave, we're over. I'm not doing this anymore."

Spinning to face him, she shakes her head. "That's not fair."

"What's not fair is you continuing to try to start drama, then getting mad when I point it out."

"I'm not starting drama. I'm asking questions." She throws her hands into the air. "We paid for this trip to grow closer as a couple. We didn't pay for this trip so Cybil and Tanner could spend a week sneaking off and hooking up."

"Tanner and I are not sneaking off and hooking up," I say in my defense, unsure if that's a lie or not, because we did share a kiss this morning after sneaking off, but I don't think either of us planned on that kiss. At least I know *I* didn't.

"Right, your lips are totally swollen." Lauren rolls her eyes, and I instantly touch my fingers to my mouth and notice that my lips do feel tender.

"I don't mind if Tanner and Cybil are hooking up," Avery says, winking at me, and my cheeks instantly warm.

"We don't care either," Jacob inserts, and I find him and Parker both sharing the same smug look.

"I don't mind, either, Cybil," Oliver says softly while Lauren huffs, crossing her arms over her chest.

"Though I appreciate all your approval, whatever happens between Cybil and me is not up for discussion, as it has no effect on me doing my job or you getting what you need from this trip," Tanner says, then locks eyes with Lauren. "If you want to leave, Maverick and Blake will take you back to the lodge when they leave. That said, I think you need to think about why you agreed to come on this trip and consider Oliver's feelings. He obviously wants you here, so maybe you should put all your energy into working through things with him."

He pulls his gaze off her and looks to everyone. "Now, I know this morning has been crazy, but everyone still needs to get dressed, gather firewood, and have breakfast. We have a four-mile hike down to the river today, and when we get there, each couple will need to catch at least two fish, clean them, and have them ready for dinner."

"What?" I feel the color drain from my face while nausea turns my stomach. I might be able to fish, as long as I don't have to touch any worms and I get to let the fish go, but there's no way I'll be able to kill or clean a fish.

"I know you don't eat meat, so I'll show you different berries and mushrooms you can forage for."

"Thank God." I sigh in relief, and he grins at me before glancing toward everyone.

"Get dressed, then hit the woods. We need more firewood if we're going to eat breakfast, and Blake and Maverick will be here in the next thirty minutes."

As everyone heads into their tents, I walk toward Tanner, and he turns his full attention on me. Once I'm standing toe to toe with him, I shake my head. "Now I see why you need to go off radar for a few days after one of these trips. Is it always this exciting?"

"Not normally." His gaze drops to my mouth, and his lips tip up. "But I'm not complaining about this trip."

"Stop." I laugh, shoving his shoulder before I start toward the woods. "We need to go gather firewood."

"Is that code for 'I want to sneak off with you and make out'?" he asks, following on my heels.

"No, it's code for 'I'm hungry,'" I say, then gasp when he takes my hand and spins me to face him.

"So you don't want to kiss me again?" he asks, his warm breath brushing against my lips while my fingertips dig into his biceps.

"I guess one more kiss won't hurt," I whisper, looking into his eyes, sure that I'll never get enough of his mouth on mine.

Chapter 9

CYBIL

Lost. I'm so freaking lost I spin in a circle as fear causes tears to burn the back of my throat. Tanner told me to stick to the tree line near the shore, so it's my fault for not paying attention to my surroundings as I wandered with my eyes to the ground, foraging like he taught me to. Stopping in place, I close my eyes and try to listen for the sound of the group, hoping I can hear Lauren arguing with Oliver or Parker and Jacob joking about which one of them is going to catch the bigger fish. Hearing nothing but the sound of birds and squirrels running through the trees, I tip my head back and open my eyes. Through the canopy of trees above me, I notice the sky between the branches is starting to disappear as storm clouds roll in.

"You've got this. Just pick a direction." I look around again, then decide to use the ever-efficient "eeny, meeny, miny, moe" tactic to help me choose which way I should go. I can't use the branch-in-the-ground trick Tanner taught us, not that it would do much good right now if I did know how, because I don't know what direction the river is and the trees are blocking out most of the sun. I spin in circles, stopping at four points; then, when I get to the "You are not it" part of the rhyme, I head to the left, since my hand is pointing in that direction.

I stop every once in a while to listen out for anyone who might be calling my name, but each time, I'm disappointed and even more freaked out when I don't hear anything but the sound of my own panting breaths and nature.

Needing a moment to think about what I should do, I lean against a tree and take a drink of water as I look around. With the light dimming and rain beginning to fall, I know it's going to get a lot colder pretty soon, so if I don't come across anyone, I'm going to have to find a way to make a shelter for the night. Letting my head fall back against the tree behind me, I drag in a few deep breaths.

I know that freaking out is not going to help me right now, and neither is crying, but that doesn't mean I don't want to do both those things.

Lifting my head when I hear a noise that sounds like someone is in pain or crying, I scan the area around me, trying to figure out where the noise came from. When I hear a deep whine, I bolt to my feet, and that's when my heart seems to stutter inside my chest. No more than fifteen feet away is a mound of what I think is dirt at first, but I soon realize it's a large elk with a huge rack sprawled out on the forest floor. Its chest is barely moving as it makes a sound I never want to hear again in my life.

Keeping to the trees, I tiptoe, trying to be as quiet as possible, not wanting to startle it, because I know that an animal in pain will lash out at anyone it perceives as a threat. Once I'm a few feet away on the opposite side of the huge animal, I peek around a tree and swallow hard when I see he has two very noticeable injuries—one just before his hind leg and another on his neck. Both of them are turning his brown fur a deep almost-black color. Not sure what to do, but knowing I can't help him on my own, I scan the area, trying to decide which way I should go for help.

I must make a noise, or he must smell me, because I hear him grunt and then turn to see him try to stand, only to give up and sprawl out once more. My heart pounds as I run from tree to tree, wanting to keep something solid between him and me as I make my way away from him slowly.

"Fucking finally," I hear a man say over the pounding of blood through my ears, and my heart soars in relief, thinking that I've been found. But then the next statements make my heart stop and my stomach sink. "I've never had to chase an elk this far or this long."

"Well, we found him. Now we need to finish him off, cut him up, and get the hell out of here before someone comes across us," another man replies as the sound of branches breaking getting closer makes me dizzy.

"No one's out here. We don't have anything to worry about," yet another voice grumbles as the rain begins to fall harder.

"Let's get this done," the third voice says, and in the next moment, my body jerks as a loud gunshot ricochets through the trees surrounding me.

Covering my mouth, I bite my palm to fight the sob that climbs up my throat while hot tears stream down my cheeks. When the three men start to talk about how they're going to skin the elk and carry it and its rack out of the area after dark, I know I need to get away. I peek around the tree and find the three older men all dressed in camo unpacking a bag of knives and other supplies.

As I listen to them talk, it becomes obvious they don't want to be caught doing what they're doing, so I really don't want them to find me out here. With them distracted, I begin to move from tree to tree, putting space between them and me while trying to be quiet—something that is almost impossible with the debris littering the now-slippery forest floor.

"Cybil!"

Hearing what sounds like Tanner shouting my name, I freeze and close my eyes. Minutes ago, I would have cried in relief hearing my name, but now? Now, I don't know what to do or how to react. I don't want to draw attention to myself, not with the guys and the elk still so close, but I also don't want Tanner to stumble across them. When my name is shouted again, I peek around the tree to where the three men were, and my heart drops into my stomach when I see they're gone, but the elk is still there.

I glance around, wondering where they could have gone, then remember they are dressed to blend in with the environment, which makes them better suited for hiding. Unlike me, in my bright-red plaid shirt that sticks out like a sore thumb. Knowing I can't stand behind this tree forever, I listen for my name, then run in that direction as fast as I can go, yelling Tanner's name at the top of my lungs. I know it's stupid to make myself a moving target, but I want him to stop coming my way. When I finally spot him and our eyes lock, relief fills his expression before concern makes his brows dart together.

"Cybil."

"Oh God." I plow into him, my voice hoarse and my throat dry, making it almost impossible to speak. "W-we need to . . . to run."

"What's going on?" He wraps his arms around me, and I try to wiggle free from his tight embrace when all I want to do is curl into his hold and pretend the last few hours never happened.

"Run. Please," I pant, then scream when a gunshot sounds and a tree a few feet away from us splinters as it's hit with a blast.

"Fuck." He shoves me to the ground and comes down on top of me, causing all the air in my lungs to leave in a rush. "What the fuck?" His arms curl around the top of my head before he somehow manages to move us both behind the trunk of a tree. "Talk to me," he orders, crouching down in front of me, sounding firm but calm as his gaze locks with mine.

"Th-three g-guys killed an elk. I . . . I don't think they were supposed to. Th-they didn't know I was there until I ran to you."

"All right, baby," he says soothingly as he smooths my hair away from my face. "I need you to listen to me." Nodding, because I'm attempting to focus on breathing and slowing my racing heart, I see his face soften. "We're going to keep low to the ground and move from tree to tree until we reach the edge of the river, then stick to the tree line until we come across the four-wheeler. Can you do that?"

"Yes," I say, and he leans in, quickly touching his lips to mine before he grabs my hand and scans the area around us. "You won't be able to see them. They're all wearing camo."

"Got it." He gives my fingers a squeeze. "On the count of three, run for that tree." He points at one about ten feet away, then counts down with his fingers, and we both take off. When we make it without being shot at, he points at another tree, then another, and before I know it, the glorious sound of rushing water greets my ears, causing relief to fill me. "Don't let your guard down, sunshine," he orders without sparing me a glance, then points to another tree and another until the river comes into view. As we start to move to the right instead of forward, I keep an eye out for the four-wheeler, praying it's not much farther. "There it is."

A fresh wave of adrenaline blasts through my system, making me shake when I see what he's pointing at, and I look around before he lowers me to sit with my back against the tree. "What now?"

Crouching down in front of me once more, he takes my face between his large palms. "I'm going to do a quick search of the area. I don't think they followed us. I think that shot they fired was a warning to get us out of there, but I want to be sure, because once we're on the four-wheeler, we're going to be out in the open."

"Are you saying you're leaving me?" I grab hold of his wrist and lock on to him with all my strength. "Don't do that. We can—"

"The four-wheeler is going to be our best option to get us to safety quickly," he says, cutting me off, and I wonder how he can be so calm right now. "I need you to trust me, sunshine."

I do trust him, but this isn't him getting me up the side of a mountain. This is me trusting that he won't get shot while leaving me behind to cower behind a tree. "I do trust you, but what if you're wrong? What if they're still following us and they see you?"

"They won't see me." He smiles like he thinks my comment is adorable. "Stay here. I'll be right back." He forces me to let him go, touches the tip of my nose with his finger, then disappears like he's gone up in smoke.

Letting my eyes close, I listen for anything out of the ordinary, but with the water just in front of me, it's difficult to distinguish between sounds. As the minutes pass, my hands start to shake. I've never felt more anxious in my life than I do right now. When I hear a branch break nearby, my eyes shoot open, and I roll to my knees and peek around the tree first on one side, then the other, not seeing anything. Then a hand wraps around my mouth from behind, cutting off the scream climbing up my throat.

Panicking, I start to rip at the arm holding me but then still when a deep voice rumbles "It's me" against my ear.

"Tanner." I spin around to face him, and when I see it's really him, I wrap my arms around his middle. "Oh God, don't ever leave me again."

"Shhh, it's okay. You're okay." He runs his hand over the back of my head as he holds the side of my face against his chest.

"Are . . . are the guys gone?"

"I didn't see them, and there were no tracks following us." He stands and takes my hand, pulling me to my feet. Once I'm standing in front of him, he pushes me back against the tree and presses his body flush against mine. "Now I need you to hold it together for just a few more minutes while we run for the four-wheeler. Can you do that?"

"Yes."

"Good girl." He kisses me hard and fast, then leans back, giving me a look that makes me feel warm before he takes my hand, and we both run for the four-wheeler.

Chapter 10

Tanner

Even with Cybil tucked against my back with her arms wrapped tight around my waist, I have to keep reminding myself that she is safe. I fucked up. She shouldn't have been able to wander so far away from where we were fishing, but I let Oliver and Lauren's drama distract me. When I realized she was gone and that she wasn't within shouting distance, I called Maverick and told him to come down on the four-wheeler and hike with the group back to camp.

Not surprisingly, everyone but Lauren wanted to help with the search, but I knew I'd be better off tracking Cybil on my own. She hadn't been gone out of sight long; I just needed to be able to focus on locating her. Now, given the circumstances, I'm glad I followed my gut. If she's right about what she witnessed, then the men who shot at us were poachers, illegally hunting bull elk, which if caught could lead to prison time and a fine of up to $20,000. Most men wouldn't take the risk, but there are some who don't believe the rules apply to them, especially when getting a bull elk tag during hunting season is like winning the lotto.

"I'm going to stop at the clearing just ahead and call Maverick," I shout over the engine, and I feel her nod against my back as her arms tighten around my waist.

When I get to the small clearing about twenty minutes from camp, I set the engine to idle and grab the satellite phone out of my pack, wait for a signal to show up, and quickly call Mav. I let him know I've got Cybil and tell him what went down so he can call the warden along with the police and have them meet us at the campsite tonight.

By the time I hang up, Cybil's body behind me has begun to shake. Lifting my shirt, I place her frozen hands against my stomach, then pull my shirt down before I take off. I know she's cold, and the fact that her clothes are soaked isn't helping. I'm also sure she's about to crash, and when that happens, I want her to be somewhere safe. As we pull into camp, all eyes come to us, but I ignore everyone standing around the fire. I don't even acknowledge them as they start to ask questions. Without a word, I turn and drag Cybil onto my lap before I get off with her and carry her toward our tent.

"Cops and warden are on the way up," Maverick says, stepping forward to unzip the tent. "It shouldn't be long." He turns his attention to Cybil. "You okay, sweetheart?"

"Y-yes, thank you." She burrows against me.

"I'm gonna get her dry and warm," I tell him, and he lifts his chin before I duck inside the tent and set Cybil on the ground.

"I don't know what's wrong with me." Her hands tremble and her teeth chatter as I remove her wet clothing before helping her into a dry shirt and tucking her into her sleeping bag.

"You're crashing, sunshine. It's normal after going through a high-stress situation. It will pass; you just need a few minutes."

"I'm so cold."

"I know." I lie down next to her and then drag my sleeping bag over the two of us, turning her into my chest, curling myself around her, and resting my lips against her forehead. "You did good today."

Her body starts to shake harder; then I hear her laugh before she tips her head back to look at me. "I did so good that I ended up lost and shot at."

My entire body tightens at the mention of a gun being fired in her direction, and her fingers come up to touch the space between my brows. "I'm guessing from the look on your face it's too soon to joke about it."

"Yeah, it's too soon," I agree. "Then again, I don't know that I'll ever think it's funny."

The truth is that seeing the look on her face as she ran into my arms when I finally found her caused me to feel fear like I've never felt in my fucking life. I wasn't worried about myself; I was worried I wouldn't be able to protect her from whatever it was that had scared her.

"Well, thank you for finding me. I don't know what I would have done if you didn't show up."

"You would have been okay." I curve my fingers around the back of her head and tuck her face against my neck. This woman in my arms is stronger than she thinks she is; she just needs to be reminded of what she's capable of.

"I'm not so sure about that. I used 'eeny, meeny, miny, moe' to choose which direction to go, and it obviously didn't work."

Groaning, I close my eyes. "You didn't."

"I did. It was cloudy, so I couldn't make a compass with a twig like you taught us, and honestly I didn't know what direction the river was, so it wouldn't have mattered anyway."

"Right. Well, tomorrow, I'll get you a compass, and from here on out, I'll make sure you know which way you should go if you get lost again."

"So we're staying here?" I hear the worry in her voice. "I thought we would be leaving tonight, after what happened."

"After we talk to the warden and the cops, Blake, Maverick, and I will have to discuss what we should do," I tell her gently while kissing the top of her head. "Whatever happens, I promise you'll be safe."

"Okay, I trust you," she whispers, and my gut tightens, because fuck it feels good to hear the truth in her voice, and it means more than I even thought it would to get that from her.

"Tanner," Maverick calls, breaking into the moment. "Blake's on the way up, and the warden and sheriff are right behind him."

"Be out in a minute," I call back as Cybil burrows into her sleeping bag.

Placing my fingers under her chin, I tip her head back and search her gaze before touching my mouth to hers, unable to help myself. "I'm sorry, sunshine, but you're going to have to get dressed. They're going to want to speak to you."

"I knew I wouldn't be lucky enough to get out of that." She sighs, and I smile before I roll away and get up.

Giving her one last look, I leave to give her some privacy to change, and I head to where the group is talking.

Maverick turns to meet my gaze as I approach. "Is she okay?"

"She's good. She'll be out in a minute," I assure him, and he lifts his chin. Really, I'm proud as fuck at how she handled everything. I know grown men who wouldn't have been able to handle a situation like that, and she did it, stayed calm, used her head, and then warned me before I could walk into something that might have cost me my life.

"Should I go see if she needs anything?" Avery asks, turning to look at the tent, and I start to tell her she can if she wants, but at that moment, Cybil emerges looking no worse for wear and as beautiful as always. Before she has a chance to make it even three steps, the entire group swarms her, asking questions and taking turns hugging her. Even Lauren steps forward to give her a hug, which surprises me—and Cybil, judging by the look on her face.

Turning back to Maverick, I cross my arms over my chest and drop my voice. "We need to figure out a plan for tonight when Blake gets here."

"I've been thinking about that. It's going to be pitch black soon, so that's going to make getting off the mountain tonight almost impossible without making multiple trips with the four-wheelers. I don't like it, but I think we'd be better off if we all stay here, and you, Blake, and I can sweep the area with the cops when they arrive. If anyone's in the vicinity, hopefully that puts them off from approaching."

"I doubt they're still out there." I look into the woods. "My guess is the shot they fired at us was meant to scare us away from where they were so they could finish what they were doing. They're probably long gone by now. That said, I don't know how comfortable Cybil is going to feel staying here, considering what happened."

"Then I'll take her down to the lodge and stay with her there," he says, and my hands ball into fists, the reaction as involuntary as the "Fuck no" I growl.

"Figured you wouldn't be down with that." He shakes his head. "Blake's not going to be happy about you and Cybil hooking up."

"Blake's going to have to get the fuck over it," I state clearly as the roar of multiple engines fills the night air. I turn to look for Cybil, finding her heading my way, and as soon as she's within touching distance, I reach for her hand and keep hold of her as the sheriff and the warden arrive with Blake.

"We're close. This is the tree they hit when they shot in Cybil's and my direction," I say, shining my flashlight on the trunk of the large fir, which has a chunk missing.

"This is fresh." Sheriff Montero bends to pick up one of the splinters from the base of the tree. "How far away did you say you were when they fired?"

"Maybe fifteen feet." I walk away with my light to the ground, looking for the place where I took Cybil down when the shot was fired. When I come across it, I look back to where the sheriff is still standing, and anger curls around my insides. I knew it was close, but now seeing the distance, which is less than I thought it was, I know that if they had been trying to kill either Cybil or me, they easily could have in that moment.

"Gotta say, son, I agree with you. They weren't trying to kill you; they were trying to scare you off."

"That doesn't make me feel any better," I tell him honestly.

"Wouldn't make me feel any better either," the warden says as he adjusts his hat.

"What direction did you come from?" Blake asks, and I glance over at him. He's been quiet ever since Cybil and I gave our accounts of what went down to the warden and the sheriff.

The only time he's spoken was to agree that it would be too much of a risk to take the group to the lodge tonight and to say he was going to ride with me to show the sheriff and the warden where everything happened, leaving Maverick at camp. I know he wants to ask about Cybil and me but is pissed about it and doesn't want to say something that will cause a rift between us, which means he'll wait until he's cooled down to bring it up. As for me, I'm giving him his time, because I'm still trying to wrap my mind around things myself. The only thing I know is I want a hell of a lot more time with Cybil, so I'm going to have to figure out how to make that happen, and I hope she wants the same thing.

"This way." I head in the direction Cybil ran from, and we all fan out and walk in a straight line without a word, everyone knowing that if they cleaned up after themselves, that's going to be the best way to find anything with almost zero visibility.

"Unless a bear took down a large elk, I'd say this is where they were when they field dressed the elk," Warden Stemson says, shining his flashlight on what's left of the entrails the hunters left behind. "Your girl said she didn't hear any four-wheelers, so my guess is they walked out." He shakes his head. "It's not going to be easy to find out who's responsible."

"I've gotta agree with Stemson on this one. It's not going to be easy to find out who did this, but we've got a few cameras on the road leading up the mountain. I'll see if I can find anything." Sheriff Montero sighs, looking around one last time before heading back toward the river.

When we reach the four-wheelers, Warden Stemson sticks his hand out in my direction. "I'll let you know if I find out anything, and if they took down the elk as a trophy, they'll want to take it to a taxidermist. I'll call around tomorrow so the ones who are local know to phone in if anyone approaches them with a job."

"Thanks." I let his hand go.

Sheriff Montero pats my shoulder. "We'll be in touch."

"Do we need to be concerned about having guests out here?" Blake asks, and Warden Stemson stops halfway to his ride and turns to face us.

"I don't think you guys have anything to worry about, but it'd be smart to move your guests to the other side of the river. I doubt the men responsible for this mess will be back, but you just never know what some of these idiots will do or what they're thinking."

"Thanks," Blake says, and I lift my chin, then wait for them to drive off before turning to get on our four-wheeler.

"What are you thinking?"

"Tomorrow, you would have moved anyway. Now you'll just set up camp in a different location than what was planned." He hops on the seat behind me. "I'm also going to ask my dad to put some feelers out. Men around here can't help but to brag when they get a bull elk, and I have no doubt that someone will slip up. For all we know, they've already posted a picture on Facebook to show off their kill."

"I doubt they'd be that stupid," I mutter as I start the engine.

"They were stupid enough to hunt out of season without a tag and to shoot at you. I wouldn't put anything past them right now," he shouts over the noise as I pull back on the throttle, anxious to get back to Cybil.

Chapter 11

CYBIL

"I can't believe you!" Lauren's high-pitched cry wakes me suddenly, and I blink my eyes open, finding the tent barely lit with early-morning light and a very grumpy-looking Tanner up on an elbow, glaring at the door.

"You can't believe me? I can't believe you," Oliver hisses back, sounding outraged.

"You haven't wanted to have sex *once* since we've been here!" Lauren yells, and my eyes widen.

"We're in a tent, not in a hotel, and neither of us has showered in four days. Of course I don't want to have sex."

"Are you saying you think I smell?" she shrieks, and I cringe, because right now, we all kind of stink, so I can't really blame Oliver for not wanting to be intimate. That doesn't mean I don't feel bad for her.

"For the love of God, shut the hell up and go to sleep!" Parker roars, and I quickly cover my mouth with my hand while I wait for Lauren or Oliver to respond, but neither of them does. In fact, the silence that follows is almost deafening.

When Tanner lies down facing me, the humor I see in his gaze makes me giggle. I know I shouldn't laugh, but it's hard not to, especially when it's like neither Lauren nor Oliver remember that people outside their tent can hear them anytime they're in there.

"Morning," he mouths, touching his fingers to my cheek, and my eyes slide to half mast as my heart starts to dance inside my chest.

"Morning," I whisper back, staring into his eyes while his thumb moves to trace my bottom lip.

"Did you sleep okay?"

"Yes," I say, while leaving out that I wasn't able to fall asleep until after I heard him come back with Blake. Even knowing he was safe, I was worried about him returning to the same location we had been shot at earlier. Honestly, I didn't want him to go back at all, but I knew there would be no changing his mind, so I didn't even bother trying to stop him. "Did you?"

"I would have slept better with a whole lot less fabric between us, but yeah, I slept all right." His grin and words cause heat to spread up my neck as his eyes roam my face. "It's cute when you blush." He reaches up and touches the bridge of my nose and down my cheek.

"I'm not blushing. I'm cold."

"You can come into my sleeping bag. I'll warm you up."

"You just can't help yourself, can you?" I laugh, rolling to my back, then turn my head to look at him. "What torture do you have planned for us today?"

"Hiking, kayaking, and more hiking." He smiles when I groan. "I thought you said you've been enjoying yourself."

"I have been, but hiking is not something I've fallen in love with, especially when we seem to be going uphill all the time."

"Today, the hike will be pretty light, and you'll have cell service where we'll be stopping for lunch, so you can make a couple of phone calls."

"Really?" I smile, excited about the idea of talking to Jade. I feel like I have so much to tell her about these last few days—not that I'm going to tell her about yesterday. I don't want her worrying about me, and I know she will.

"Really." He gets up on his elbow and smiles down at me before leaning in and brushing his mouth over mine. "I'm going to check the fire and start coffee."

"I'll get up and start packing." I wrap my arms around his neck, wanting another kiss, and he grins, giving me what I want, so I let my arms fall away.

"Do you want coffee?"

"Yes, please." I sit up as he unzips his sleeping bag.

As he stands, I watch his muscles move under his smooth skin as he grabs his cargo pants to pull them on, then bends to grab a fresh shirt and put it on over his head. Once he's dressed, he puts on his boots, gives me a smile that makes me feel tingles in a few different places, and ducks out of the tent. When he zips the door closed, I imagine a scenario just like this, only with him leaving me in a big comfy bed while going to a kitchen to make coffee; then I remember that won't be happening, and my heart sinks into my stomach.

Tomorrow will be my last morning waking up with him, since the final day of our trip will be spent at the lodge, where we'll be celebrating making it through the week with dinner, a night of relaxing, and sleeping in rooms there. Dropping my face into my hands, I close my eyes. I don't know how or when, but somewhere along the way, I forgot this situation is temporary. In just a few short days, I'll be going home, and when I do, things between Tanner and me will end just as quickly as they started.

"Darn." I sigh, feeling beyond disappointed as I crawl out of my sleeping bag. I really need to be careful over the next couple of days, unless I want to go home with my heart more of a mess than it was when I got here. I just hope I'm not too late, because the truth is I've already started falling for Tanner. I like spending time with him, I like the way he makes me feel safe while pushing me to try new things, and in the very short time we've known each other, I've grown accustomed to the easy affection between us. But if I let things continue on, I won't know up from down.

Sitting in a kayak, with Oliver in the seat in front of me, I try to ignore the heat I feel coming from my left, where I know Tanner and Lauren are. I decided not to waste any time putting my plan to keep my heart safe into effect this morning. I thought that it would be almost impossible to stay away from Tanner, since he's my partner, but Oliver and Lauren's constant fighting gave me the excuse I needed.

Instead of listening to them argue, like I've done every day, I suggested that Lauren and I switch partners. Oliver agreed immediately, while Tanner, on the other hand, was less than pleased with the idea, and Lauren looked about ready to scratch my eyes out.

"I was going to guess that, since you asked to switch with Lauren today, things were not working out between you and Tanner. But the contemplative looks he keeps sending your way tell me that's not the case," Oliver says quietly, dragging me from my thoughts, and my paddle skips over the top of the water before I adjust my hold so it glides through the surface once more.

"Umm." I chew my lower lip, not sure how to respond.

"What happened? Did you two have a fight?" he asks, looking at me over his shoulder.

"No, we didn't fight. Nothing happened. I just thought—"

"Is it your ex?" he says, cutting me off, and I shake my head.

"No, it has nothing to do with my ex." I rub my lips together, then admit, "I just realized that I don't live here. I don't even live close. This whole thing . . ."

"You realized that you could get hurt," he fills in, and I nod, then realize he can't see me.

"Yes," I whisper, my stomach rolling at the reminder.

"When my ex and I met, she lived in Oklahoma, and I lived in Seattle. We spent our first year together in a long-distance relationship; then I proposed, and she moved in with me. If it's meant to be, you can make it work."

"I guess you're right, but I've only known him a couple of days," I say softly, not sure that he's the best person to accept advice from. I've overheard Lauren talking, and from what I understand, Oliver and his ex are not even divorced, and yet he's here with Lauren, trying to work on their relationship, which seems a little backward to me.

He turns to look at me over his shoulder once more, his gaze locking with mine. "I know I'm not the best person to give advice," he says, obviously reading my mind. "But trust me: you should talk to Tanner about how you're feeling. I think you might be surprised by what his response is, and you shouldn't worry about how long you've known each other; there's lots of time for that, and no one stays the same forever, so you'll be learning new things about him all the time."

Before I can reply, he twists back around, and I glance over at Tanner, finding him watching me. Like always when our eyes lock, my stomach flutters and my pulse races. Pulling my gaze off his, I look down at the water and chew the inside of my cheek. Maybe Oliver is right; maybe I should just be honest and tell him how I feel. Then again, I'm not sure I can trust how I feel; plus, he might think I'm a complete loon for bringing up what's bothering me, when we've only just met.

As we slowly make our way across the lake, I go back and forth on what I should do, and I still have no idea as we paddle up to the small inlet where Maverick is waiting for us. Before I even have a chance to make it out of my kayak on my own, I find Tanner at my side, taking my paddle before helping me out. I start to thank him, but the look he sends me has me slamming my mouth closed.

"You good with these guys for a few minutes while Cybil and I talk?" Tanner asks Maverick while locking on to my wrist as I try to move away.

"Yep." Maverick lifts his chin; then his eyes come to me, and he raises a brow. I shrug before Tanner starts to tug me toward the tree line beyond the bank.

"Is everything okay?" I ask, but he doesn't even acknowledge my question. Instead, he leads me farther into the woods, so deep I can no longer hear the group talking. "Are you not going to answer me?" I question, starting to get nervous; then, the next thing I know, he's directly in front of me, and he's cupping my face gently between his large hands.

"I'm glad you want to talk, sunshine, because I really want to know what the fuck happened between the time I left you all sweet looking and smiling in your sleeping bag this morning, and when you came out of the tent looking like someone killed your puppy." My heart stutters in my chest.

I thought I had done a good job hiding how I was feeling. Apparently, I didn't, and he is obviously mad—really, really mad—judging by the way his jaw is clenching.

"I don't know what you're talking about." I swallow, and he lowers his head, bringing our faces so close together that his nose brushes against mine.

"Don't start lying to me now, Cybil. Tell me what happened."

"Okay." I lift my hands between us and rest them against his chest, rubbing my lips together. "I realized I'm leaving in just a couple of days, and when I do, this, umm . . . this thing between us is going to be over. So I'm thinking it might be better to put some distance between us before someone gets hurt." I feel nauseous and wonder if he knows the person who is going to end up hurt is going to be me.

"Is that what you want? You want this to be over when you leave and to just give up before we really have a chance to explore what this is?" he asks softly, and my chest starts to feel funny as my nose starts to sting. Gah, even just the idea of not seeing him after this makes me want to cry.

"No." I swallow again.

"Can you stay in town for a few days after this trip?" he asks, and I nod, because I totally can. "Do you want to stay with me for a few days?"

"Yes," I say softly, and the look in his eyes makes me realize that maybe he has been hurt too.

"Then that's the plan, and we will figure out the rest." He rests his forehead against mine. "Sunshine, did you really think I would let you go so easily?"

"I didn't want to get my hopes up," I admit, and he skims his thumb across my jaw right before he kisses me gently. And just like that, I don't know up from down, but I also can't bring myself to care.

Sitting next to the lake, with my hoodie up over my head to ward off the chill in the air, I watch the water ripple against the rocks as I dial Jade's number. When I hear Avery laugh behind me, I smile; then my smile grows when Jade answers with a loud "Oh my God, Cybil. I've called you a million times!"

"Sorry." I laugh, picking up a small pebble and tossing it into the lake. "We haven't had phone service until today."

"Are you okay? Are you having fun? What have you been doing? Tell me everything," she rattles, and I shake my head.

"I'm good, for sure having fun, and there's so much to tell you, but I don't have the time today. We just stopped for lunch, and this is the only time I'll have cell service until we get back to the lodge the day after tomorrow. Are you okay? How are things there?"

"I'm good. Things are good," she says; then she pauses before adding quietly, "I had lunch with Galvin yesterday."

"Oh." I drop my eyes, not sure what to say.

"He got married," she blurts, and I blink, positive that I heard her wrong.

"What?"

"I told myself that I would wait to tell you when you got home, but I just . . . I don't want you to find out from someone else, or on social media, since it's all everyone is talking about." She takes a breath as I stand and make my way farther down the beach. "He . . . God, Cybil, he married Chris in Vegas the day you left for Montana."

"Chris," I repeat, trying to wrap my mind around what she's telling me. "Chris—his roommate from college Chris?"

"Yes," she confirms, sounding unsure.

"Oh." I close my eyes as things begin to fall into place.

His third year at college, he got an off-campus apartment, and that's when he met Chris. He broke up with me twice the first year of them rooming together, and I was not allowed to stay with him when I went to see him. Then a few months ago, he went to spend a week with Chris in Seattle—something he did every couple of months. When he came home, things seemed different between us. There was a distance that wasn't there before, and he stopped wanting to be intimate.

I didn't really dwell on it too much, because I knew he was busy and I was too. Plus, planning the wedding of his mom's dreams was stressing us both out. God, I was so stupid. It also now makes sense why Chris seemed to hate me so much.

"His parents disowned him," she says, and I take a seat as my chest starts to ache. I've known his mom and dad since I was a kid, and they are both very traditional. They always have been. Unlike some parents, who might come to accept their child when they open up about their sexuality, I doubt they will, which makes me wonder if that's why he was with me.

"Is he okay?" I ask quietly, even knowing that he's not and unsure if I should care. He's always tried to do everything his parents expected him to do, and I'm sure he's devastated that he had to choose between making his parents happy and doing what he knew would be right for himself.

"He's upset. He hates that he's hurt everyone, especially you. But . . ."

"But he's happy," I finish for her. "I'm glad for him. I mean, I'm pissed that he obviously lied to me for God knows how long, but I'm glad that he's doing what's right for him, that he's finally being honest."

"God, I fucking love you," she whisper-hisses, and tears fill my eyes. "I told him that you would understand once you knew. I mean, I know you might not ever be friends again, but I knew you would still want him to be happy."

"I will always want him to be happy," I tell her quietly as I watch Tanner walk toward me carrying two plates of food.

"He'll be relieved to hear you don't hate him."

"I could never hate him," I reply truthfully, dropping my eyes to the ground and trying to process everything I'm feeling. "I'm going to eat lunch. We'll talk when I get back to the lodge. I love you."

"I love you too. Call as soon as you can," she says before she hangs up, and I tuck my phone into the pocket of my sweatshirt, then try to smile as I accept a plate from Tanner.

"Everything okay?" he asks, taking a seat next to me.

"That was my best friend, Jade. She had lunch with my ex yesterday," I tell him, and his body next to mine seems to fill with tension. "He . . . umm . . . got married the day I drove here."

"What the fuck?" His eyes lock with mine, and I shake my head.

"He married his college roommate, who happens to be a guy," I add, and his eyes widen slightly. Dropping my eyes from his, I pick up my sandwich that moments ago I would have devoured, but right now, the heavy weight in my stomach is making me feel sick.

"Are you okay?" he asks softly, touching his knuckle under my chin, and I meet his gaze.

"The truth?" I prompt, and he nods. "I'm hurt, not because he's found someone, but because he lied to me. I'm angry with him for not being truthful with me, but I'm also relieved, because if he had kept his secret and married me, we would have both ended up miserable. I also . . ." I swallow. "I'm also wondering if he was cheating on me, if he cheated on me every time he went to meet up with Chris. The thought makes me want to be sick."

"Cybil." His voice sounds gruff as he wipes at the tears I feel soaking my lashes.

"I'm so mad, but I also feel bad for him, which is making it difficult to be angry." I drag in a deep breath through my nose.

"What do you mean?" he questions softly, studying me closely.

"His mom and dad are very old school. I doubt they'll accept him being married to a man, and he loves his parents, so I know he's probably hurting. Even as mad as I am, I don't want that for him."

"If they love him, they'll learn to accept him however he is. Like you said, he lied, and I'm guessing he's been lying for a long time. They might be upset right now, but they need time to figure out their feelings and come to terms with things. That said, what he did to you was wrong. Even if he wasn't sleeping with someone else while you were together, the fact that he had an emotional relationship with someone else is fucked up."

"You're right," I whisper, and he wraps his arm around my shoulders and rests the side of his head against mine. "Is it wrong that I really wish I could kick him in the nuts?"

"I don't think so," he chuckles, and I smile, thinking that even though it's weird to lean on him right now, it also feels really fricking right.

Chapter 12

Cybil

Sitting around the campfire, with the lake just a few feet away and the stars glittering above me, I realize I'm going to miss this. Before this trip, I never would have thought I would fall in love with the great outdoors or camping, but this trip has given me a different perspective. It's pushed my limits, forced me to try new things, and reminded me that I'm capable of doing just about anything.

This trip has also given me a chance to reflect on myself and my relationship with Galvin that I wouldn't have had if I hadn't come. There's something to be said about unplugging from everyday life. It gives you the opportunity to just listen to your inner voice, which you don't always have when you've got technology at your fingertips.

Then there's the man sitting next to me with his pinkie wrapped around mine. If I hadn't come on this trip, I wouldn't have met Tanner, so I might actually owe my ex a thank-you.

But only after I kick him in the balls.

"I have a great idea," Lauren says loudly, pulling me from my thoughts, and everyone sitting around the campfire stops talking and turns to look at her. "I think we should all go skinny-dipping."

"Lauren." Oliver shakes his head. "We are not going skinny-dipping."

"Why not?" she pouts. "It's our last night out here. We should do something fun as a group."

"Getting naked together isn't really my idea of group fun," I say dryly, and Parker, who's sitting on the other side of me, snorts.

"Don't be a buzzkill, Cybil." Lauren rolls her eyes while she stands and whips her shirt off, leaving her in her sports bra. "I'm going in, and whoever wants to join me can join me."

"I wouldn't suggest you do that," Parker says, but of course she ignores him and walks off.

"Oh wow, she's serious," I whisper, watching her strip off her clothes before she runs naked toward the water.

"I guess I should go grab a towel for her." Oliver stands with a shake of his head; then, a moment later, I hear a splash and turn to look at the lake.

"One thing can be said for that girl. There's never a dull moment with her around," Avery says as I watch Lauren's head appear right before she dives under again.

"Ain't that the truth," Jacob agrees as we all watch Oliver make his way down to the water, carrying a towel and muttering under his breath.

"Oh my God!" Lauren lets out a bloodcurdling shriek before she starts paddling wildly toward the shore. "Something touched me!"

"It was just a fish," Oliver tells her calmly while holding open the towel for her as she runs out of the water and into his arms.

"It didn't feel like a fish, Oli," she cries, clinging to his neck when he scoops her up. He starts murmuring quietly to her while carrying her to their tent.

"How much do you want to bet that we're going to hear them going at it for the rest of the night?" Grant grumbles, and my nose scrunches.

He's probably right; Lauren might not have taken an actual shower, but she's now cleaner than any of us. And if that was the only thing stopping Oliver before, he might feel better about it now.

"Well." Avery pushes up off the ground and looks at her husband. "I'm going to bed, and with any luck, I'll fall asleep before any of the vocals start."

"Be there in a minute," Grant tells her, and she nods before saying good night and making her way up the bank to the grassy area where we set up camp.

"I think I'm going to try to do the same." I get up and say a quiet good night to the guys, and Tanner gives me a look that says he wants to kiss me but can't.

After I quickly brush my teeth, I change into a pair of sweats and a hoodie, then get into my sleeping bag with my headlamp and my book, hoping that reading will distract me from the chill in the air. Tanner won't come to bed until everyone else has called it a night, so I still have a while before I can shamelessly take advantage of him for his body heat. Something I've done the last few nights—not that he seems to mind.

In fact, I think if he had his way, we would squish ourselves inside one sleeping bag. My stomach flutters at the idea of him and me actually sharing a bed and having time alone within four solid walls. Really, I'm a little nervous about what will happen when we head back into the real world. I don't know if we'll even still like each other. I don't know how the chemistry between us will translate when it comes to being intimate, and my experience with men is limited to Galvin, so I don't know how to be with anyone else. And again, Tanner and I don't know each other well, so I'm really trying to trust my gut, which has led me wrong in the past.

And then there's the fact that I'll have to leave to go home.

When anxiousness starts to replace the excitement I was feeling moments ago, I open my book. If I spend too much time dwelling on what might or might not happen, I'll talk myself out of taking a chance, which I know I'll regret in the long run, and with this last week as proof that sometimes trying something new can change everything, I don't want to do that.

"Cybil."

I spin around in my sleeping bag and then hold my hand to my chest.

"You scared me," I tell Tanner as my heart pounds under my palm.

"I called your name about five times," he says; then his eyes move to the book I dropped. "You didn't hear me. I'm guessing you were at a good part."

"Yeah." I pick it up and flip back to where I left off, then dog-ear the page to save my spot.

"So what's happening now? Did Katharine come around?" he asks.

"You remembered her name?" I laugh, and he stops what he's doing to look at me and shrug.

"I guess."

"Well, Edward is not really giving Katharine a choice, and even though he's all gruff and badass, he's sweet with her, which is breaking down her walls."

"Good for him."

"Yeah," I agree as a shiver slides down my spine.

"Cold?" he asks. He changes into a pair of flannel pants and a long-sleeved shirt that molds to his body like a second skin.

"Yeah, it feels colder tonight than it has this week."

"'Cause we're on the lake," he says. Then he orders, "Get up and hand me your sleeping bag." Frowning, I do as he asked. As I jump around to keep warm, he unzips my bag, then his, and after a few curse words, he zips our bags together. "Now climb in." I do, and a moment later, he gets in with me. "Now, come here."

I hesitate for only a moment before curling myself into his side, the position much more intimate without our sleeping bags between us. As I lay my head on his chest, he tugs my leg up over his hip, causing a mass of sensations to flood my system. My belly clenches, my pulse starts to race, and heat rushes between my legs. Lord have mercy, I don't know if I'll be able to stop myself from hyperventilating.

"Relax, sunshine." His warm breath feathers against the top of my head, and I wonder if it's possible to have an orgasm from just touching and if your hair is supposed to be an erogenous zone, because it feels like it is. Maybe I have nothing to worry about when it comes to us taking things to a new level, because I never felt like I do now with Galvin.

"I *am* relaxed," I lie through my teeth.

"Right, you feel really relaxed." He laughs, then says, "Hand me your book."

"Why?"

"Just hand it to me," he repeats, so I reach behind me to find it and hand it over. With my head against his chest once more, I watch him open to the page I left off on and then listen to him begin to read. Hypnotized by his deep voice and the feel of his fingers smoothing back and forth across my spine, I melt against him.

"No one's read to me since my mom did, when I was little," I tell him quietly, and he stops, making me regret opening my mouth. I expect him to say something to that, but instead, he just kisses the top of my head, then goes back to reading.

I close my eyes to fight back the sting of tears that simple gesture brings on, then move my hand to rest over his heart, which is beating steadily—unlike my own, which is going wild.

"Harder, Oli!" Lauren's cry breaks into the moment; then my eyes widen in surprise as she moans, "Just like that."

"Fuck me," Tanner grumbles.

"We can all hear you!" Parker shouts, and I cover my face, embarrassed for them.

"Christ," Tanner groans, and I burrow into his side as laughter I can't control crawls up the back of my throat. "I can't fucking wait until this trip is over," he says against my ear.

I snort my agreement while Lauren moans louder.

~

Huffing and puffing as we walk up a steep incline, I try to remind myself with every step I take that we're getting closer to this day being over. I knew today would be the hardest of the trip. Tanner, Maverick, and Blake kept warning us it would not be easy, but I assumed that since we've been hiking every day, it would be the usual torture.

I was wrong.

We started off the day hiking, followed by kayaking, then lunch, and now more hiking, only now we've been moving mostly uphill over rocky terrain for about four hours. My legs and arms feel like they're on fire, and my feet are killing me. If it weren't for the hot shower and bed awaiting me at the end of this, I would have given up a few miles back. But honestly, even with all the pain I'm in, I'm sad this trip is almost over. It's been fun experiencing new things, eating under the stars in front of a campfire, and sharing time with people who've become my friends. The good thing is I know that this doesn't have to be my last adventure. I now trust myself to take risks and experience life outside my comfort zone.

"I don't want to sound like a six-year-old stuck in the back seat of a car, but are we almost there yet?" Avery whines, breaking into my thoughts, and I smile at my feet.

"Not much longer," Tanner says, reaching out to catch me when I stumble over a root sticking out of the ground along the path.

"Thanks," I mumble, not risking lifting my eyes off my feet to look at him.

"We have about a mile before we reach the road where Maverick will pick us up."

"Thank you, baby Jesus," Parker says with a sigh. "My legs are about to give out on me."

"Well, I think today's been great," Lauren chirps. "Don't you think today's been great, Oli?"

I barely hold back a giggle. Maybe not surprisingly, Lauren has been in a great mood all day. She hasn't complained once, and she and Oliver have gotten along better than they have this entire trip. Honestly, I wish they'd slept together earlier in the week.

"It's been a great day," I hear him agree.

"Stop rubbing it in our faces that you two got laid," Parker says, and the entire group laughs.

"You're just jealous," Lauren says, making me wish we had Freshly Laid Lauren with us this entire trip instead of Angry Sex-Starved Lauren, who found every reason to be unhappy. Then again, maybe this trip has brought Lauren and Oliver closer together too; maybe being out here has made them realize why they're together. Whatever it is, I'm glad they're getting along today.

"Truth," Jacob agrees.

"I see the road!" Avery shouts in a few minutes, and like an idiot, I lift my head and trip. Unlike all the times before, Tanner doesn't have a chance to catch me, and I go down hard. As I land, pain shoots through my left hand, so much pain that I'm barely able to hold myself before I face-plant.

"Oh no." I drop my forehead to the ground, and tears I can't control fill my eyes while I tuck my hand against my stomach.

"Let me see, sunshine." Tanner sits me up and takes hold of my wrist, and I open my hand, feeling suddenly dizzy when I see the large gash across my palm and blood—lots of blood. "Shit." He whips his backpack off while Lauren and Oliver both start ordering me to hold my hand above my head.

"I think I'm going to be sick." I swallow the saliva filling my mouth, watching blood drip on the ground in front of me.

"Close your eyes and breathe." Lauren pats my back.

"It will be okay. Tanner's going to clean you up, then we'll get you to the hospital for stitches," Oliver tells me, holding on to my wrist tightly.

"Slow and steady—everyone get up to the road and let Maverick know what's going on," Tanner orders the others, who wish me luck before complying.

"Do I really need stitches?" I peek one eye open to look at him as he dumps water over my open palm to clean away the dirt and pine needles.

"Yeah, sunshine."

"Figures this would happen right when I get to the finish line," I grumble, closing my eyes.

"You still did great today."

Shaking my head, in too much pain to laugh, I peek one eye open once more and glare at him. "You say that every time I mess up."

"You didn't mess up. You tripped, and you did do great today, babe," he says as he wraps white fabric around my wrist before he starts to circle my hand with it over and over. "Okay, that should keep the bleeding to a minimum until we get to the hospital." He stands, then looks at Oliver. "I'm gonna give you my bag, so I can carry Cybil. Are you good with that?"

"Of course." Oliver takes his pack as my eyes widen in horror.

"That's not necessary." I take a step back from him, waving my stump-looking hand out in front of me. "I'm okay," I lie. My hand might be the worst of my injuries, but my ankle feels like it might buckle each time I attempt to put weight on it.

"Cybil—"

"Tanner, it's not far. I'll be okay." I take one step, then another, and my jaw clenches so tight that I'm surprised I don't crack some teeth.

"You're not okay." He takes my elbow when I try to pass him. "You're in pain and you're limping. I'd rather not have you tumble down the fucking mountain because you're being stubborn."

"I'm not being stubborn." I try to cross my arms over my chest, but with the bandage, it feels awkward, so I give up. "I'm too heavy, and if you try to carry me, we're both likely to end up rolling down the mountain."

"This isn't up for debate." He turns his back to me. "Hop on."

"No."

As he turns to look at me, his eyes meet mine. "Hop on, or I'm tossing you over my fucking shoulder."

Between the cursing and the look he gives me, I know he's not going to give up, so I let out a deep breath. "I can't believe I'm doing this," I mumble as I hop onto his back and wrap my arms around his neck, careful not to choke him. When his hands wrap around my thighs and he starts to move, I say a silent prayer and squeeze my eyes closed.

"You good, or do you want me to take over?" I hear Maverick ask, and I open my eyes and find him at our side as we climb the side of the mountain.

"I got her," Tanner tells him, not even seeming to breathe heavy, which I have to admit is pretty impressive.

"If you've got your phone on you, call Blake and tell him to meet us on the way with my truck. I'll trade him and take Cybil to the hospital so the group can get back to the lodge."

"Got it," Maverick says; then I listen to him relay the message to Blake as we walk up to the road. When we reach the bus, I expect Tanner to put me down, but of course he takes the steps up, and everyone starts to ask if I'm okay. As he lets me down in the front, I assure them I'm fine. The bus starts to move, forcing everyone to take their seats.

"You doing okay, sunshine?" Tanner asks, sitting next to me and wrapping his arm around my shoulders.

"Just wonderful." I rest the side of my head against his chest as he takes my injured hand in his and holds it carefully in his lap.

"How much pain are you in on a scale from one to ten?"

"One million," I only slightly exaggerate. With every beat of my heart, the throbbing pain in my hand only seems to grow more intense.

"You'll feel better soon." He turns his head to kiss the top of my hair. "As soon as we get to the hospital, I'll make sure they give you something for the pain."

"Thank you." I close my eyes, then sigh. "At least it wasn't my right hand, right?"

"Right," he agrees, not sounding like he agrees at all. "Do you have your ID and stuff in your pack?"

I frown, then lift my head to look at him. "I don't know what I did with it. I don't even remember taking it off."

"Lauren took it from you." He looks over his shoulder and calls out for her to pass the pack forward. When he has it, he sets it at his feet, and then the bus starts to slow. Not long after that, he's lifting me into the passenger seat of his jacked-up truck and driving me to the hospital.

Totally awesome.

Not.

Chapter 13

TANNER

As I sit in the chair next to Cybil, my teeth grind as I attempt to keep my cool, something that Dr. Smooth—yes, that's really his name—is making nearly impossible for me to do. Before now, I never understood why men act like Neanderthals around their women, pounding their chests and growling one-syllable words. Now, I fucking get it, and it will be a miracle if I make it through Cybil getting her stitches without acting like a jealous asshole.

"I travel to Oregon quite frequently. We should meet up the next time I'm there and have coffee," Dr. Smooth says with his head tipped down, completely missing the daggers I'm shooting at the side of his head.

Cybil licks her lips, glancing at me quickly. "Maybe," she says, and the only reason I don't toss a chair, pound my chest, and war-cry the word *mine* is because she looks a mix of bewildered and a little horrified by the attention and suggestion.

"Cool." He looks up at her, smiling, with his shaggy blond hair falling into his eyes. "And if you're going to be here a few more days, I could show you around."

"She'll be with me," I say, unable to help myself, and he turns my way.

"Oh." His brows draw together as he focuses back on Cybil. "I thought you said you were just here for one of those adventure trips."

"Buddy," I growl, and his eyes fly to me, "can you just focus on stitching up her hand? She's tired and not interested."

Swallowing, he drops his gaze and gets to work. Thankfully, he's quiet while he finishes up, then quickly provides instructions on how to take care of the injury and when to return to have the stitches removed. By the time we leave the hospital, the sun has set, and Cybil is half falling asleep. I stop at the drugstore to pick up her prescriptions and then drive to the lodge, when all I really want to do is take her up to my place and hide her away for the next week, maybe even longer.

"Do you think everyone will be mad if I just wave at them and go to bed?" she asks after I open the passenger-side door to my truck.

"Even if they are, who the hell cares?" I turn so that she can climb onto my back, ignoring her huff before she wraps her arms around my neck and her legs around my hips. Thankfully her ankle is fine, but she did twist it, so it's going to be sore for a couple of days. "And you need to take a pain pill."

"I know. I also want to shower, but I don't know that I'll be able to do that with this stupid thing." She holds her bandaged hand in front of my face. "It's going to take me a year to wash my hair."

"I'll help you," I assure her, feeling the muscles in her thighs tense under my palms. "I'll also keep my eyes closed."

"Yeah, right." She laughs, and I smile as I head up the steps and walk through the door. Before I even have a chance to put her down, Parker spots us and tells everyone we're back, so Cybil is engulfed and slammed with question after question. I watch as she's helped to one of the couches, then lift my chin to Blake and Maverick as they make their way across the room toward me.

"We need to talk," Blake says, walking past me and right out the door. I look to Mav, who shrugs, giving me a look that states clearly he doesn't know what's going on, before we both follow Blake outside.

"I talked to our lawyer," Blake says, spinning to face us, and my spine stiffens as my eyes narrow. "He assured me that the contract Cybil signed is pretty much ironclad, so she can't sue us. But he said it might be smart to have her sign something to say that the accident was not our fault."

"Pardon?" I narrow my eyes, sure I heard him wrong.

"Look, I get that you're into this girl, but we need to protect our business and not get caught up with pussy."

"What the fuck did you just say?" I take a step toward him but stop when Mav's hand comes to rest against my chest.

"Brother." Mav shakes his head at me.

"We had a deal when we started this business." Blake takes a step back. "We agreed that there would be no fraternizing." He crosses his arms over his chest. "I'm not willing to lose everything because you got the hots for a client and can't keep your dick in your pants."

"First." I lift my hand and point my finger in Blake's face as rage runs hot through my veins. "Do not *ever*"—I accentuate each word—"fucking *ever* again refer to Cybil as 'pussy.' Second, what the fuck I do with my dick has never been and will never be any of your business. And third, we are equal partners, so you should fucking know that I would never do anything to jeopardize what we've built."

"You've been distracted since the day she showed up here," he says in defense while looking at Mav for his agreement.

"And?" I stand back and cross my arms over my chest. "Did anyone complain about the job I did during this last guide?"

"No." He frowns. "But that's not the point."

"So what is the point? I didn't plan on Cybil showing up. I didn't know her before this trip. But I gotta tell you, man, I will fucking walk if you try to make me choose between her and this place." I startle myself with that statement, but even as freaked as it makes me, I know it's true. No one has ever made me feel what she has in the short time that I've known her, and as much as I love the people I consider family here, they are not *mine*, and if I'm right about Cybil, she's going to be that to me—*my family*.

"You don't even know her." His nostrils flare, and his fists clench.

"The point is, I want to *keep* getting to know her. Fuck, man, you know me." I shake my head, disappointed as fuck and pissed the hell off. "You've known me for years. You should know this is something else, and the fact that you want to act like I'm thinking with my dick is fucked up and complete bullshit."

Blake looks at Mav once more.

"Sorry, man, but I gotta agree with Tanner on this." Mav steps back so he's no longer between us. "I'm not saying I'm happy that Cybil is a client, but I know Tanner would not go there unless he felt like there was something between them."

When Blake doesn't say more, I sigh. "If we're done here, I need to get Cybil to eat something so she can take her meds. And in the morning, I'm heading to my place with her. If you need me, you know how to get ahold of me." Then, without a backward glance, I head inside and straight to Cybil.

"Is everything okay?" she asks as I carry her down the hall to my room. When we built this place, we knew we'd each want to have a space of our own to crash after a trip, or when we had to be here early before a guide. So we built a separate wing at the back of the lodge with three small studio apartments away from the guests, which is nice after coming off a long week.

"All good." I set her on her feet when I reach my door, then quickly type my code into the lock and let us in. "I'm going to go get your suitcase from your car and something for you to eat," I tell her as I help her over to the couch in the corner of the room. "The TV works, and the password for the internet is Livelifeadventures, all one word with a capital *L*, in case you want to go online." I grab my laptop, which is still on the bed where I left it the last time I was here, and hand it over to her.

"I can go get my bag." She starts to stand but stops when her eyes meet my narrowed ones. "Okay." She lifts her hands. "I won't go get my bag, but something seems off with you. Is everything okay?"

I close the distance between us and take her face between my palms. "Everything is good." Really, it's better than good, even with the bull-shit. It feels right having her in my space, having her with me. "I just want you to eat something, shower, and take your pill so you can rest. It's been a long fucking day." I brush my lips across hers.

"I really am okay." She leans back to look me in the eye.

"Liar," I say quietly, seeing the pain she's trying to hide. "I'll be right back. Relax." After she nods, I take off, first going to her Bronco to get her bag, then stopping in the kitchen to pick up a tray of food. When I get back to the room, I find her curled up on the couch, watching some history documentary on the television.

"Did you know that the first chain saw was invented to help make it easier for doctors to remove babies from women?" she asks as soon as I enter the room.

"No."

"Well, it was. How horrifying is that?"

"Pretty fucking horrifying," I agree, carrying her food and a bottle of juice to the couch and handing her the plate. "Eat, so you can take your pill and shower."

"Please." She raises a brow.

"Sorry." I smile. "Please eat, so you can take your pill and shower." I sit next to her with my own plate of food.

"I know you said everything is fine, but I noticed that you, Blake, and Maverick talked, and since then, you seem to be on edge," she says when a commercial comes on. "Do you want to talk about it?"

"Blake isn't happy about you and me."

"Oh." She sets down her fork and starts to bite her bottom lip.

"He's just worried. Live Life Adventures is his baby, so he's just concerned about us spending time together and how that could affect business."

"I'm sorry. I don't want you guys to fight because of me," she says quietly.

"You have nothing to apologize for," I reply, and she starts to fiddle with a loose thread that's hanging from her shirt, not looking convinced. "Mav, Blake, and I are family. I don't have brothers or sisters, and my parents aren't in my life. Mav has a similar story to mine." I set down my plate on the coffee table in front of me and scrub my hands down my face. "The three of us might disagree from time to time, but at the end of the day, we have each other's back." I turn to look at her. "Blake will come around after he pulls his head out of his ass."

"Okay," she agrees, still not looking convinced, then winces when she moves her hand.

"Pain pill, shower, then bed." I push off the couch and take our plates to the small kitchen, dropping them in the sink. Then I take her one of her pain pills before I grab a rubber glove, along with a roll of medical tape.

"I think I'll be able to manage showering on my own." She looks around at anything but me as I take a seat next to her and start placing the glove on her hand.

"How about you do what you can, then shout for me if you need help?"

"Yeah, okay, thank you."

"No problem, sunshine." I tape the glove tight enough around her wrist that water won't be able to get into it. "All set," I say, and she stands, going to her suitcase to dig out a makeup bag and a fresh set of clothes before heading for the bathroom.

"Be right back," she says with her cheeks turning pink.

"I'll be here if you need me."

With a nod, she closes the bathroom door; then a moment later, I hear the shower turn on. Not long after that, I hear her start to grumble.

"Tanner," she calls, and I walk toward the door as she opens it just enough to peek out. "I can't get my sports bra off." The tears I see in her eyes make my gut clench.

"Step back and let me in," I say gently, and she moves, letting me into the room. Then, without a word, I turn her so that her back is to me. "Lift your arms."

"This is so humiliating."

"It's not," I assure her, and she groans before lifting her hands over her head. I grab the tight material at her sides and carefully maneuver it over her breasts, then head. "Do you want me to help you with your pants?"

"No." She crosses her arms over her chest and turns to face me. "I think I can get them off on my own." She glares at her hand. "Hopefully."

"All right, I'll be outside."

Not surprisingly, she doesn't ask for my help again, but she does stay in the shower for close to an hour. When the door opens and she steps out wearing a baggy shirt and shorts, the scent of vanilla filling the small space, my mouth waters at the sight.

"Feel better?" I take her hand and unwrap the tape before removing the glove.

"Yes, but now I'm exhausted." She yawns. "I'm sorry for taking so long. I had to wash my hair about ten times before it felt clean."

Smiling, I run my eyes over her long, wet blonde hair and pretty face and see that she looks more relaxed than she did. "The pill kicked in."

"Yeah." She yawns again. "Between that and today, I feel like I could sleep for a year."

"I bet." I motion to the bed for her to climb in, then go to the TV and swivel it around before I hand her the remote and steal a kiss. "I'm gonna shower."

"I'll be here." She lies down, and I give her one last look before I step into the bathroom and close the door.

Fifteen minutes later, clean and wearing a pair of basketball shorts, I step out of the bathroom to find Cybil already asleep. Exhausted myself, I turn off the lights and crawl into bed next to her. I turn off the TV, then maneuver her until she's lying half on me, careful to place her hand on my chest.

As her warm breath brushes against my skin, I close my eyes, relishing how fucking perfect she fits against me and how easily I've come to care for her. Unlike her, I've never had a serious relationship. When I was young, girls tended to stay away. I grew up poor. My parents would spend what little money the government sent them each month on booze instead of on the kid they didn't want. That meant I didn't have more than one change of clothes, showering was a rarity at times, and food was scarce.

I joined the military when I turned eighteen, and ever since then, I've been focused on making it so that any kids I might have one day will never have to struggle like I did. Women for me have been a fun distraction from time to time, but never more than that. With Cybil, things are different. There's no denying the chemistry between us, but it's more than that for me. I crave her presence, and how at peace she makes me feel when I'm around her, and there's no denying the urge I have to protect and take care of her. Something she seems to need from me, and something easy for me to give her because I've never had someone who needed that from me before.

I let out a deep breath and hold her a little tighter. Fuck, but I'm really looking forward to having her all to myself for the next week.

Chapter 14

Cybil

"Told you he was into you," Parker whispers in my ear as his arms tighten around me, and I laugh. "I'm happy for you two."

"Thanks." I smile as he passes me to Jacob, who hugs me just as tightly. Then I step back into Tanner, who wraps his arm around my waist. "I'll call you guys and let you know when I'm driving home, so we can meet up for lunch or something."

"We'd like that," Jacob says softly, watching stupid tears fill my eyes. "Do *not* cry."

"I'm not going to cry," I deny, even though I've been a weepy mess all morning. "I think I might be allergic to the pain meds."

"Sure." He smiles as Parker and Tanner both laugh. The truth is I had no idea it would be so hard to say goodbye to everyone. Oliver and Lauren were the first to leave this morning. I wasn't too broken up about them going, but I still got emotional. Then Avery and Grant took off, anxious to see their son, and I cried like a baby. Now I feel the tears coming on again, and I'm not sure I'll be able to hold them back.

"We'll see you in a few days." Parker closes the distance between us, dropping a kiss to my cheek before looking at Tanner and patting his shoulder. "Take care of her."

Tanner doesn't respond, but he does lift his chin, which I'm guessing is his badass way of agreeing.

"Drive safe, guys." I wave at the two of them as they get into their Jeep, then watch as they back out and drive off with a honk.

"Are you okay?" Tanner asks, turning me to face him, and I nod, then drop my forehead against his chest. "Tired or pain?" His arms slide around me.

"A little of both." Even after going to sleep early, I still feel like I could sleep for a year. The pain in my hand was relentless all night and kept waking me up. "I'll take a pain pill after we get to your house."

"I got some water for you in my truck. You can take one on the way."

"I'm driving, so I don't think that would be smart."

"You're not driving." He gives me a squeeze.

"Yes, I am." I tip my head back to look at him and frown at the look he's giving me.

"You're not."

"I am."

"Cybil, you can barely use your hand, and your ankle is fucked up. You don't need to be driving. You can ride with me, and I'll sort out someone to drive your Bronco up to my place later."

"I'm fine." I cross my arms over my chest and match his glare with one of my own. "I can drive myself to your place; then you won't have to worry about getting someone else to take time out of their day to deliver my car to me."

"You're not driving." He glares, and I press my lips together, because it would be rude to laugh in his face.

"You are not the boss of me, Tanner. I want my car with me," I say, and he studies me for a long moment. He must see I'm not going to give in, because he lets out a loud disgruntled sigh.

"Fine, I'll drive your car. My bike is at home. I'll ride it down and pick up my truck later."

"Really?" I roll my eyes. "Tanner, that is not necessary. I can just follow you."

"No, either you ride with me, or I drive your Bronco. You choose."

Letting out a frustrated huff, I give in and toss him my keys. "Fine, but if you hurt Sammy, you and I are going to have problems."

"I don't think Sammy would notice even if she was rolled off a cliff," he says, looking at her rusty and dented exterior with his lip curled.

"She was my mom's, so I would notice," I inform him.

Understanding fills his gaze, and his expression softens. "Right, I promise I'll take good care of her," he assures me, walking to the passenger side to let me in. "I'm going to get my bag and shit from my truck. I'll be right back." He gives me a swift kiss before slamming my door. As I wait for him to return, my cell phone vibrates, and I open it up to find multiple messages from Jade asking if I'm okay. Instead of sending her a text back, I dial her number and listen to it ring as Tanner puts his stuff in the trunk.

"You know, it's really annoying that I can't just drive out to your house to check on you when you don't answer your phone," Jade greets in my ear, and I smile.

"Sorry, I ended up having to get stitches yesterday, and by the time I got back to the lodge, the only thing I wanted to do was shower and sleep."

"You had to get stitches?" I hear the worry in her voice. "What happened?"

"Long story short, I tripped, fell, and cut my hand open. I'm fine, though," I assure her.

"You've always been clumsy, so I'm not even a little surprised. So when will you be home?"

"Umm . . ." I look at Tanner as he opens the driver's side door and gets in. "In a week."

"Oh. I thought you planned on driving back today."

"That was the plan before, but I'm going to spend a week with Tanner and—"

"Sorry," she says, cutting me off before I can explain who Tanner is. "What did you say? I think I heard you wrong. It sounded like you said you were spending a week with a man named Tanner."

"That's what I said," I say as he starts the engine, which transfers the call to the car stereo system. Sammy might be old, but she has been updated a lot, just not on the outside. "Please don't start freaking out."

"You're going to stay in Montana for a week with a man you don't know, and you don't want me to freak out?" Jade's voice rings through the interior, and I smile awkwardly at Tanner.

"I do know him," I say with a sigh, trying not to get frustrated with her. "I just spent an entire week with him. He's not some random man I met at a bar."

"Okay, but you still don't know him, Cybil, and this is so not like you. I mean, is this because Galvin and Chris got married?" she asks, and Tanner's hand on the steering wheel tightens, turning his knuckles white.

"Are you kidding me?" I take a breath to make sure that I choose my next words wisely. "I agreed to this week with Tanner before I even knew about Galvin and Chris, so no, this isn't because of them. I'm staying because I really like him. I like spending time with him, and I'm not ready to leave yet. Plus, I planned on taking two weeks off, so I don't have to rush home."

"Mom and Dad are going to lose their minds," she says, and I can picture her rubbing her forehead or stomping around in her store.

"Probably," I agree, not looking forward to calling them and wondering how long I can put it off. "Then again, they were okay that time you snuck off to Cabo with that guy you met at the airport when you were supposed to be coming home from seeing your grandma. So even if they are mad, they'll get over it eventually."

"That and this are not even close to the same thing," she hisses as Tanner drives us down the tree-lined dirt road away from the lodge, moving one hand to wrap around my thigh.

"How is this any different?"

"Because you're Cybil. You don't do wild shit like that, and I don't even know this guy. He could be—"

"You're on speakerphone right now," I say, cutting her off before she says something that will embarrass me more than I already am. "And I'm not doing anything wild. I'm spending more time with someone I just spent a week with."

"You're spending time with a man," she says, seemingly unconcerned that he can hear everything she's saying.

"Yes," I agree. "And?"

"You've never even talked to a man besides Galvin before. Sorry, but this is all a little much for me."

"I was always with Galvin, so I had no reason to," I point out.

"You've lost your mind," she whispers, and I let my head fall back against the headrest. One thing I haven't missed this last week is everyone questioning my judgment and thinking I can't make decisions for myself.

"You need to trust me," I reply.

"Cybil, this is—"

"Jade, I love you," I say, cutting her off again. "But I'm not a child, so please stop. You're not going to change my mind."

"Okay." She sounds somewhat stunned, then is quiet for a long moment. "Will you at least send me his information?"

"She can do that." Tanner glances over at me as he gives my thigh a squeeze.

"Thanks, *Tanner*." She laughs, sounding disgruntled.

"I'll be fine, and I'll call your mom and dad so you don't have to break the news to them."

"Dammit, Cybil, I knew I should have gone with you," she grumbles. "I knew you'd go to Montana and find a cowboy with a deep voice and never come home."

"Tanner isn't a cowboy. He's a former marine, and I didn't say I wasn't coming home." Truth be told, I have no idea what will happen after this week, and really I don't want to think about it, because the thought of this not working out makes me feel anxious, especially after realizing that you can know someone for years and have no idea who they are.

"Even worse," she gripes. "Just promise you'll call me."

"I promise I'll call you."

"All right," she agrees, then calls out, "Tanner!"

"Yeah."

"If you don't take care of my best friend, I will drive to Montana, track you down, and kill you in your sleep."

"Right," he says, his lips twitching into a smile that causes his dimple to pop out.

"I'm serious."

"I promise I'll take care of her," he says, glancing over at me, and my entire chest warms from the look he gives me. Right, it's those looks that remind me exactly why I'm taking this risk.

"Good, and Cybil? You'd better call Mom and Dad. I'm not dealing with that mess."

"I'll call them."

"Love you," she huffs.

"Love you too. I'll call soon." I press end on the call, then tuck my cell back into my bag. I know I said I would call her parents, but I didn't say when, and I have no desire to hear them lecture me with Tanner here for the conversation.

"She loves you."

"Yeah. She's also a little overprotective."

"She's worried. It's understandable, and you're lucky you have people who care." He gives my thigh another squeeze, and I cover his hand with mine. "You're tight with her parents?"

"They were my mom's best friends." I let out a breath as I fiddle with his fingers. "When Mom passed away, they took me in, and I lived with them until I was old enough to be on my own." I lift my head to look at his profile. "What about your family? Are they going to freak out that you have a woman staying with you who you don't really know?"

"I haven't seen or talked to my parents in nine years," he says, and my chest starts to ache. "When I turned eighteen, I joined the military and didn't look back."

"Tanner," I murmur, not sure what to say, not even sure that if I said something, it would be enough.

"They didn't want kids; they didn't want to do anything but party all night and sleep all day. I was an inconvenience."

"I hate that for you," I say as the ache in my chest causes my eyes to burn.

"Don't." He glances over at me while his fingers lace carefully through mine. "As fucked up as they were, I wouldn't be where I am now without them," he tells me quietly, then shakes his head. "I've made a life for myself, have friends who are like family, got money in the bank, and do a job I love. Because of them and in spite of them, I've succeeded."

"Well, I'm proud of you," I tell him, giving his fingers a squeeze. "And not in the way you're proud of me for doing nothing but walk up a hill," I say, and he chuckles, the sound easing the pain around my heart and the lines around his eyes.

"Thanks, sunshine."

"Anytime," I say, shifting to look out the windshield.

"We're here." He flips on the turn signal and turns onto a dirt road lined with tall spruce and pine trees.

At the sight of a log cabin–style home with a large arch of windows and a wraparound porch, my breath catches in my throat. I never tried to picture where he might live, but if I had, it would have been a cool condo or something similar. Not this. The home in front of me looks like the house I grew up in, the wooden structure blending in with its surroundings and making it feel like a piece of the landscape instead of standing out.

"This is where you live?"

"This is it." He sounds nervous, so I turn to face him.

"It . . . it's beautiful." I bite my lip, then shake my head. "I have to show you something." I dig through my bag until I find my phone, then quickly search my photos until I find the one I'm looking for. "Here." I hold out my cell to him, and he takes it, studying the picture I took, looking confused. "That's my house in Oregon, or the house I grew up in."

"Seriously?" His eyes meet mine, and I nod, my throat tight.

"How wild is that?"

"Wild," he agrees, looking out the windshield before dropping his gaze to the photo once more. The two homes that are thousands of miles apart look almost identical, which should be impossible but is obviously not. Another connection we didn't even know we shared. "I designed this place myself," he says, sounding like he's talking more to himself than me.

"My mom spent a year drawing up designs for our house. The builder threatened to quit at least once a week, because she could never make up her mind on what she wanted." I smile as a million memories come back to me and then take my phone back, studying the photo. "All she cared about was the light. She was an artist at heart." I look at him and swallow when I see the look in his eyes.

"How about we go inside?" he suggests, and I nod, watching him get out of Sammy, and then a moment later, he opens my door and lifts me out. Taking his hand, I walk with him toward the front porch of the cabin, then stand back as he types in a code and opens the door.

I step in when he motions me to enter before him and am slightly disappointed when the place looks nothing like the house I grew up in. The walls are bare instead of covered with paintings and photos, and the wood floors are naked rather than covered with random mismatched rugs to keep out the cold. After setting down my purse on the island in the kitchen, I go to the open living room and turn in a circle. Where the house I grew up in was worn from time and use, everything here is new and modern. Top-of-the-line appliances fill the kitchen, high-back barstools line the counter, and a comfortable-looking gray-suede L-shaped couch takes up most of the large living room in front of the fireplace, where the TV is hung.

"I love it." I stop turning and look out the windows into the forest, noticing a big building tucked into the woods with two glass rolling bay doors. "What's that?"

"My bike, a couple of four-wheelers, and some of the backup equipment for the lodge." He comes to stand at my side. "I'll show you around the property later, but for now, I'm gonna get you your pill. While you rest, I'm going to take my bike down to pick up my truck and go to the grocery store, since the fridge is basically empty except for a couple of eggs."

"I can drive you," I tell him, and he gives me a look that has me holding up my good hand. "Or not."

"Yeah, or not." He leans in, touching his lips to my forehead. "Be right back." He turns and heads outside, and a few minutes later, he returns carrying my bags and his. He takes them down a hall, then reappears holding my pill bottle.

"Thanks." I meet him in the kitchen, where I take my pill and the glass of water he hands to me.

"You wanna hang out here, or do you wanna lie down in bed and try to sleep?" he asks as I swallow the pill down.

At the reminder that I'll be spending the week in his bed, my face warms, which is ridiculous, given the fact that I've already slept beside him every night since I got here. "If the pill hits me like it did last night, I'll probably fall asleep." I hold up my hand. "Dr. Smooth said the pain would only last a couple of days. I hope he's right, because I hate taking these pills and sleeping so much."

"It just happened yesterday. It's going to take a day or two for the pain to become manageable. Right now, rest is the best thing you can do to heal."

"I guess." My nose scrunches. "This just isn't how I thought we'd spend the first few days of our week together," I say, and his eyes seem to darken, which sends a thrill down my spine. Besides kissing, he's kept everything PG—something I appreciate, even if it is making me a little antsy.

"It's just day one." He pushes away from the counter. "Anything special you want me to pick you up from the store while I'm there?"

"Veggies, fruit, yogurt, snack bars, those kinds of things." I dig into my bag for my wallet and grab what cash I have, holding it out to him.

"I'm not taking your money." He frowns at my hand with the same frown he gave me earlier when we were arguing about me driving myself here.

Here we go again. "Tanner, I can pay for my own food."

"I know you can, but you're not going to." He takes the cash and tosses it toward my bag, and I watch it fly across the counter and teeter on the edge. "I'll show you the room, then hit the road."

"You did not just do that." I shake my head in disbelief as he drags me behind him down the hallway.

"Sunshine, I don't want to spend the next ten minutes arguing with you about taking your money, especially when I'm not going to do it. I'm skipping that argument so I can go and get back here."

"Great. I'm already learning something about you," I tell his back.

"What's that?"

"You're unbelievably annoying." I sigh as he pushes open the door to his room and stops just inside.

"You're just upset you're not getting your way. You'll get over it." He grins down at me, then points to a door off to the right of the king-size four-poster bed that matches the two dressers and side tables. "Bathroom is through there, TV remote is next to the bed, and your stuff is in the closet if you want to change." He turns toward me, cups my face in his large palms, and kisses me, making me forget I was annoyed with him just a moment ago. "I shouldn't be gone long."

Licking my lips, I nod, and his eyes drop to my mouth, causing my belly to dip.

"Rest up. I'll be back." He touches his lips to mine once more quickly, then lets me go and heads out the door. With nothing else to do, and already feeling sleepy from the lack of sleep last night and the pain pill, I slip out of my flip-flops, crawl into his bed, and fall asleep with a smile on my face.

Chapter 15

CYBIL

As the smell of something delicious filters through my sleep-addled mind, my stomach rumbles and my eyes flutter open. It takes a minute to remember where I am, and when I do, I sit up and search for a clock. Not finding one in sight, I look to the window, noticing that the light outside has dimmed drastically.

Pushing my hair out of my face, I get up and head to the bathroom, and after taking care of business, I wash my good hand and check out my appearance. The braid I put my hair into this afternoon is falling out, and my mascara has smudged under my eyes. I pull out the tie and undo the braid, which leaves my hair a mass of waves, then wipe the mascara off the best I can.

With nothing to do about the wrinkles covering my thin cotton T-shirt dress and too lazy to change, I leave the room barefooted and follow my nose to the kitchen. I find Tanner wearing a pair of basketball shorts and a white tee, standing in front of the stove. Like he senses me, he turns, and a smile lights his eyes. "I figured if I started cooking, you'd wake up."

"You were right." I step up to his side and rest my head that still feels heavy on his shoulder, and he wraps his arm around my waist. "What are you making?"

"I called Blake's mom to get some ideas for dinner when I was at the store, and she gave me a simple recipe for fajitas that she promised I couldn't fuck up."

Laughing, I tip my head back toward him while my heart melts that he took the time to call someone and find out something to cook for me. "Well, it smells delicious." And it does. Between the peppers, onions, mushrooms, and seasoning, my mouth is watering.

"Let's hope it tastes as good as it smells." He leans in for a kiss, so I lift up on my toes, meeting him halfway. "Did you sleep okay?"

"Yeah, but I slept a lot longer than I thought I would."

"You were tired." He shrugs, then lifts his head and frowns when there's a loud knock on the front door.

"Expecting someone?"

"No." He hands me the spatula he was holding. "Can you keep an eye on this?"

"Sure." I take it, and he kisses the top of my head before leaving the room. A moment later I hear the front door open, then what sounds like a woman speak. Feeling something uncomfortable settle in the pit of my stomach, I set down the spatula, then quietly peek around the corner and watch an older woman with dark-brown hair that's cut into a stylish bob place a few plastic containers into Tanner's hands. She then reaches up to pat his cheek affectionately.

"You can come in and meet her," Tanner says, turning in my direction, so I duck back quickly and rush to the stove, pretending I wasn't just spying on him. A second later, the two of them appear around the corner, and I know instantly that the woman is Blake's mom. They might not have the same hair color, but her eyes and features are almost identical to her son's.

"Cybil, I'd like you to meet Janet, Blake's mom. Mom, this is Cybil," Tanner says, setting the containers on the island, completely missing the way her face softened when he called her Mom.

"It's so nice to meet you." I smile as Tanner comes around to take the spatula from me. "Tanner told me that you're responsible for all the delicious food I ate this week. You're an amazing cook."

"It was fun trying some new recipes, so I'm glad you enjoyed everything." She motions to the containers. "That's why I stopped by. There were some leftovers and dessert from last night that I didn't want to go to waste."

I don't believe her, not even a little. My guess is she heard I was staying here, and like any good mama bear, she came to check me out and see what her cub was up to. And honestly, that makes me like her even more, especially after finding out today that Tanner didn't have that in his life growing up.

"Thank you, it won't go to waste," I say, and she nods; then her eyes drop to my hand.

"How are you feeling today?"

"Better. The pain pills are kicking my butt, but I'm definitely better than I was yesterday. Tanner's been taking good care of me."

"I'm sure he has been." She smiles softly, then glances at the watch on her wrist. "Darn, I need to get home to make dinner myself before Dave burns down the house. It was nice meeting you, Cybil. I'm sure I'll see you this week for dinner." She looks to Tanner for confirmation.

"We'll set it up," he assures her, and she nods. Then, after a quiet goodbye, Tanner walks her to the door. When he comes back a few minutes later, I can't help but laugh. "What?"

"You do realize that she only stopped by to make sure you didn't invite a crazy woman to stay with you, right?"

"No, she didn't," he denies with a shake of his head.

"She totally did." I take a seat on one of the barstools, and he looks toward the door, seeming surprised by the thought. "It's sweet that you call her Mom."

"Yeah." His expression gentles. "When Blake, Mav, and I would get time off, we'd come here, and after about the third visit, she started insisting we call her Mom. We didn't fight her on it. She's a good woman."

"She loves you."

"The feeling's mutual." He shrugs like it's not a big deal, but I know it is, especially given his relationship with his own parents. "Are you ready to eat?"

"Yes." I start to stand but stop when he shakes his head.

"Stay. Just tell me what you wanna drink. I have pop, water, and juice. I've also got beer and wine, but you can't drink with that pill."

"Juice, please." With a nod, he grabs two plates, setting them on the counter before taking beans and tortillas from the oven and sour cream, salsa, and cheese from the fridge. Once he has everything laid out, he pours us each some juice, then takes a seat next to me. "Thank you for cooking."

"Anytime." He turns his head my way and leans in, so I smile and touch my mouth to his.

An hour later, stuffed full, I watch from the stool I haven't been allowed to move from as he shoves the dishes into the dishwasher, and I somehow manage with a whole lot of willpower not to tell him he's doing it wrong or to cringe when he doesn't rinse things off. "Are you sure you don't want me to help?" I ask, watching the gunk-covered pan go into the dishwasher, and he gives me the same look he's given me every time I've asked. "Okay, do you mind if I call Jade's parents?"

"You don't have to ask if you can make a call, sunshine. You just can't help me clean up." He grins, pushing my bag toward me, and I roll my eyes as I listen to him chuckle. Once I find my phone, I ignore the messages on the screen and dial Maisie's number.

"Cybil, honey," she greets softly after the third ring. "I've been anxious for you to call and check in."

"Sorry, we didn't have service. Then yesterday, I had a little accident."

"Oh no, are you okay?"

"Yeah, I just have a new set of stitches."

"Child, you're so clumsy. What did you do this time?" she asks, and I smile at her exasperated tone.

"The usual. I tripped over my own feet and fell. Only the rock I landed on wasn't happy about it."

"How many stitches this time?"

"Six." I study my palm, which is now an ugly shade of purple and green.

"So less than the time you fell down the stairs and more than when you decided to cut a frozen chocolate cream pie with a butcher knife."

"Yeah," I say with a laugh.

"Well, I'm glad you're okay." She sighs. "So besides ending up in the hospital again, how was your trip? I know you were nervous about going."

"It was really good. I learned a lot and actually had fun."

"That's good. I'm glad you had a good time." I hear her moving around; then she asks quietly, "Do you know when you'll be home?"

I glance up at Tanner, and my stomach flutters. "In a week or so. I'm . . . well, I actually met someone here, so I'm going to spend some time with him before I head back."

"You met someone on a couples retreat?" I hear the frown in her voice.

"He was our guide. His name is Tanner, and he and I were partners all week. He—"

"Did Jade tell you about Galvin?" she says, cutting me off before I can tell her how great he is and how much I like him.

"She did."

"I knew she wouldn't keep quiet about that. I told her not to tell you until you got home. That girl never listens."

"Maisie—"

"Honey, people are going to say what they want to say. You can't run away from this. You're going to have to come home eventually."

"I'm not running away," I say to defend myself, disappointed that she thinks I would; then again, maybe I haven't given her much of a reason to think differently.

"Honey, you spent the last few months since Galvin ended things locked in your shop. I get it—we all get it—but you can't live like that, pretending things aren't happening when they are. You didn't do anything wrong. You have nothing to be embarrass—"

"Maisie, please stop," I interrupt while dropping my eyes to the top of the island. "Please listen to me. Really listen to me."

"Okay, Cybil, honey. I'm listening."

"I met someone I, like . . . really like, and I'm spending a week with him. I know that, given what happened with Galvin and Chris, it's easy to assume the two things are related, but they are not. I'm spending a week with Tanner because I'm not ready to leave him yet, and he's not ready for me to go."

"Cybil—"

"Maisie, I'm asking you to trust me."

"Okay," she says, giving in quietly, and I let out a relieved breath.

"Are . . . are you sure about this guy, honey?" she asks, and I meet Tanner's gaze, and as I look into his eyes, I know that no matter what happens, I want to see where things might go between us.

"Yeah, I'm sure."

"Okay," she whispers. "I love you."

"I love you too. I'll call you tomorrow."

"Tell him to take care of you."

"I will." My shoulders sag as I end the call.

"That bad?" Tanner asks as I drop my forehead to the top of the counter.

"Not bad. It would just be easier for people to accept that I'm here with you because it feels right if Galvin hadn't just gotten married. Right now, everyone is assuming that I'm staying because I don't want to go home and deal with that situation." I lift my head, and he takes a seat next to me and wraps his hand around the back of my neck, smoothing his thumb up and down.

"It's mostly my own fault," I whisper. "When Galvin ended things, I was embarrassed and hurt, so I lost myself in work and stayed out of town. I didn't want to deal with the questions I knew people would ask, especially when I didn't have any answers." I shake my head, then drop my elbows to the counter and pull my hair back from my face.

"Hey." He takes hold of my chin, forcing me to look at him. "You had a reason to be upset. You didn't do anything wrong." His eyes scan over my face; then his eyes lock on mine. "Your family is worried. I'd be concerned if they weren't." He pulls me forward until his forehead is touching mine. "They will come around, but in the meantime, I'm happy you're here. I want you here with me."

"I want to be here." I lift my good hand and rest it against his jaw.

"Then let's just be, and we'll figure the rest out when it's time."

"Okay." I nod, closing my eyes as his lips press to mine; then his tongue skims my bottom lip, and I open for him. As one of his hands slides into my hair and the other curves around my waist just under my breast, I latch onto his shirt, ignoring the pain in my hand as I make a fist.

"Tanner," I breathe when he drags his mouth from mine so he can skate his lips down my throat. My knees between his press together and heat pools in my lower belly, making me dizzy with desire.

"Shit." He pulls back suddenly, and my eyes flutter open as he removes my hand from his tee so he can inspect it. "Damn, sorry, sunshine. Let me get some gauze." He gets up, and I notice my hand is bleeding, not a lot, but I definitely opened part of the wound. When he comes back over, he takes my hand and wipes it down before wrapping it with clean gauze. "How does it feel?"

"It's okay, honestly. I didn't even notice," I say, and he gives me a look that causes the space between my legs to tingle.

Bringing my hand to his mouth, he kisses it. "I'm going to have to be careful with you."

"I'm not that breakable."

"I know." He pulls me up to stand. "Do you want a pill?"

"No." I shake my head, not wanting to fall asleep again.

"All right, how about we watch a movie?"

"Sure." I force myself not to pout. Gah, I really want to, because all I want is for him not to be careful and take me to bed.

"Come on." He leads me to a door just off the kitchen, and when he opens it, we step out onto a covered porch that's fully screened in. Fairy lights line the perimeter, with a U-shaped couch in the middle. When he lets my hand go, I watch him pull a screen down from the ceiling, then open a box and pull out a remote. "What are you in the mood for?"

"Anything, I'm not picky." I watch him press some buttons on the remote, and warm air starts to blow down on us; then the large screen lights up.

"Romance, comedy, or action?"

"Do you want my real answer?" I ask while I take a seat.

"Romance it is." He smiles, and a list of romance movies fills the screen.

"You don't have to suffer because of me. I'll be happy with anything." I curl into his side when he sits next to me.

"Choose, sunshine." He passes me the remote, and I study it, surprised that he's just handed it over. The guys I've known have treated the remote like some kind of weapon of mass destruction, not to be trusted in the hands of a woman. "Cybil."

"Sorry, I'm just trying to figure out if I'm worthy of this kind of power," I say, and he laughs, wrapping his arm around my shoulders.

Resting my head on his chest, I scroll through until I find something I haven't seen before and then press play. As the movie begins and the couple on screen struggles to get to know each other, I relax into Tanner and start to wonder if it's abnormal to feel this level of comfort with someone you just met. I mean, I know we spent a week together, but we still haven't known each other very long. And besides the underlying current of sexual tension that seems to surround us all the time, things between us are easy.

"What are you thinking about so hard?" he asks, breaking into my thoughts, and I stop twirling my hair.

"Nothing."

"Liar." He takes my hand when I sit up and then kisses my fingers. "Is your hand okay?"

"Yeah." I chew the inside of my cheek, then blurt out, "Is it always like this?"

"Like what?"

"Easy." I motion between us. "I mean, I don't know; it feels like things are really easy with you."

"Should they not be?"

"I don't know," I repeat. "It's not like I have a lot of experience with this kind of thing."

"Do you want me to give you the cold shoulder and then start chasing you because I finally realize how special you are?" he asks with a smile, basically relaying what's happened so far in the movie we're watching.

"No." I roll my eyes.

"Maybe we should stop watching this movie before you take off back to Oregon because we have some stupid misunderstanding, only for you to have to beg for my forgiveness."

"How do you know that you wouldn't be the one begging for my forgiveness?"

"Because I would never do something to fuck this up," he states plainly, and my heart gives a funny thump.

"Neither would I," I say, and he pushes my hair back away from my face, tucking it behind my ear.

"I'm sure, given time, we'll find shit to fight about and piss each other off. So right now, let's just appreciate how uncomplicated this is."

I bite my bottom lip, then let it go and nod. "I think that's smart."

"Good." He smiles as he drags me forward for a kiss, and I sink into him, getting lost in the moment of his tongue touching mine. Needing to be closer, I climb onto his lap with his help. "Keep your hand here," he orders, capturing my wrist and placing my wrapped palm against his hard chest. "Move it and we stop." He leans up, nipping my bottom lip.

"I won't move it," I vow; then I feel his hand on my ass as he drags me forward, which means his hard-on that's barely restrained by his thin shorts hits me right between my legs. My breath catches, my core clenches, and wetness spreads right . . . there.

"You okay?" His hand moves up over the curve of my ass.

"Yeah." I rock against him without thought, and his eyes darken.

"Come here." He lifts his head enough to nip my bottom lip.

"I'm right here," I pant against his mouth before nipping his bottom lip like he did mine. Then his fingers thread through the hair at the back of my head, and he urges my mouth down to his as I rock against him again.

"I can see you're going to be a test of my willpower."

"Why do you say that?" I ask, but instead of answering, he thrusts his tongue into my mouth before biting and licking my lips while his hand on my ass travels around to cup my breast. Out of pure instinct, I press closer and rub myself against him. I have never been this turned on, and I'm pretty sure I might cry when he slows the kiss and pulls back.

"Your hand."

"Sorry." I wince when I find that my hand has moved up to his hair and is gripping it tight enough to cause me pain.

"I might have to tie your wrist to the bed for your own good," he says, and a shiver of excitement travels down my spine while a smile that can only be described as devilish curves his lips. "But not tonight." He leans up to kiss me swiftly, then carefully helps me off his lap. As he rewinds the movie and I settle into his side, I try my best not to pout, but I know I don't succeed when he glances at me and laughs.

"It's not funny."

"Sunshine, trust me when I say this hurts me more than it hurts you." He adjusts the bulge in his pants, making me feel somewhat better. "That said, I'm not going to risk you opening your wound back up."

Knowing he's right, I sigh, ignoring the feel of him shaking in silent laughter while hiding my own smile by tucking my face against his chest.

Chapter 16

Cybil

Standing in the kitchen with a cup of coffee in hand and still half-asleep, even after my shower, I watch in a daze as a shirtless Tanner does burpees on the back patio. As his muscles bunch and move under his tan skin, all I can think is it really should be illegal for a man as hot as him to work out half-naked, especially when he has a sexually frustrated woman staying in his house.

Hearing my cell phone that's plugged in on the counter ring, I force my eyes off the man who's captured my attention and pick it up, frowning when I see that Galvin is calling me. Part of me wants to let the call go to voice mail, but curiosity has me sliding my thumb across the screen and putting it on speaker, since I can't hold my phone and coffee at the same time.

"Yes?"

"Cybil," he says, sounding unsure, like he's forgotten the sound of my voice.

"Yes?" I repeat as my eyes drift out the window to Tanner, who's now hanging upside down from a bar, doing sit-ups.

"Umm . . . how are you?"

"I'm fantastic." I wait for him to say more, because honestly I have no desire to ask him how he is, or any other niceties. Not after finding out that he lied to me.

"Jade said you're in Montana and that you met someone there."

"I am, and I did," I agree, dropping my eyes to my feet as annoyance with my best friend makes my hand tighten around my coffee cup.

"Fuck, Cybil, I know you're pissed about everything that happened between you and me, but do you really think that's smart?"

"The only thing me being here has to do with you is that I booked this trip because you wanted us to go on a couples retreat to work on our relationship. When, in reality, there was nothing I could do to make you happy, because I don't have a penis. Besides that, you do not factor into me staying in Montana with Tanner."

"I didn't think you'd actually book that trip," he groans. "You've always hated anything to do with the outdoors, and when I brought it up, you laughed."

"I thought you were joking, and you're wrong. I actually love the outdoors." Okay, *love* might be the wrong word, but still. "I've had the best time."

"Cybil, we're all worried about you. You're staying with a man you don't even know, and—"

"Ha!" I snort, cutting him off. "That's really funny, coming from you."

"What is that supposed to mean?"

"I was with you for years, Galvin. You were one of my best friends, and I obviously had no idea who you were."

"That's not true. You knew me. You still know me."

"You didn't tell me that you were actually in love with someone else, or that you might also like men. I'm pretty sure I didn't know you at all."

"Things with Chris were complicated, and I was scared that—"

"You lied. You dragged me into your lie without giving me a choice in the matter. I mean, how long would you have let it go on for? How many times did you sleep with Chris when you went to visit him? Did you even care how I would feel?"

"I know I messed up."

"You did." My stomach churns at the fact that he didn't deny sleeping with Chris.

"Jade said you weren't mad at me." Concern fills his tone.

"No, what I said is that I don't hate you. And I don't. But that doesn't mean I'm not still really fricking pissed off at you."

"I'm sorry I hurt you. I still love you; that hasn't changed. I just . . . I just couldn't marry you."

"Well, thank you for doing one thing right." I let out a deep breath. "If that's all, I need to go," I say, annoyed with him for calling me about Tanner and mad at myself for feeling bad about being angry with him.

"Cybil—"

"Bye, Galvin." I hang up before he can say more; then my coffee cup is taken from my grasp and warm arms wrap around me, pulling me into a sweaty chest.

"Your ex?" Tanner asks as my arms go around his waist, and I rest my cheek on his chest.

"Yes." I nod, closing my eyes. "He talked to Jade and wanted to call and warn me against staying with a man I don't know," I say, more annoyed than I was yesterday at hearing the same thing from Maisie and Jade. I just wish they would trust me, trust that I can make decisions for myself.

"That was nice of him."

"Super nice," I agree sarcastically while leaning back to meet his gaze, catching his grin before his expression turns speculative.

"Are you okay?"

I don't know if it's the softness of his tone or his fingers massaging the base of my neck, but I realize the tension I was feeling just seconds ago is gone. Completely. "Yeah."

"Good." He lifts my hand between us so he can inspect my wound.

"It's feeling a lot better today," I assure him as he kisses near the stitches and rests my hand against his chest.

"I need to shower and make a few phone calls, but after I'm done, how about we head into town for breakfast?"

"That sounds good."

"I shouldn't be more than an hour." He leans in to give me a swift kiss; then, when he leans back, his eyes roam my face. "Are you sure you're all right?"

"Positive."

"Okay." He lets me go with one more kiss, this one on my forehead, before he heads down the hall toward his bedroom.

When he disappears out of sight, I take my coffee out onto the back deck along with my phone and go through my emails. I'm happy to see I have more than thirty orders waiting for me to process when I get home, along with over a dozen new reviews and messages from people who've gotten their new bags while I've been away. By the time I'm done checking all my social media accounts and replying to texts from friends, forty minutes have passed, so I head inside to get ready to spend the day with Tanner, trying not to dwell on the fact that my time here in Montana already seems to be passing too quickly.

Wearing high-waisted cutoff jean shorts, a washed-out rock-and-roll tee, a thin floral-print shrug, and wedge sandals, I hold on to Tanner's hand like a lifeline as he leads me to a table in the Root, a small restaurant tucked against the side of a mountain on the edge of town. With most of the patrons dressed casually in jeans and T-shirts, including the man at my side, I'd think my bohemian style and wild mass of wavy hair would draw curious looks from the people calling out hello to Tanner as we pass. But I have a feeling it's something else. It's like they've never seen him with a woman, which would surprise me, given how amazing he is. It also makes me wonder if my assumption is true.

"Hungry?" Tanner asks as I slide into the booth, and he takes a seat next to me.

"Starving," I say as he passes me one of the menus that was handed to him when we walked in. "What's good here?"

"Everything."

"That's helpful." I smile.

"All right," he says, laughing. "If I were you, I'd go with the cornmeal pancakes with honey-pecan butter, or the Nutella crepes with fresh strawberries."

"I've never had cornmeal pancakes." I tip my head his way. "Are they good?"

"Delicious, and the iced coffee here is better than that place down the street with the green sign I saw you eyeing when we drove by."

"I'll believe that when I taste it." I lean into him when he places his arm around my shoulders. "What are you going to order?"

"The southern omelet. Fresco, the guy who runs the kitchen here, makes his own chorizo and green salsa, and I swear it's like eating a miracle."

"They need to start paying you for advertising." I watch him grin before his attention is captured by a very pretty woman with dark hair, and his smile turns familiar. As she approaches the table with a pen and pad of paper in her hand, I notice the roundness of her stomach and wonder who she is.

"Hey, Tanner." She smiles at him, then looks at me with warmth filling her gaze. "I'm guessing you're Cybil."

"Umm, yeah." I'm sure my expression is startled.

"Blake's my twin brother." She surprises me, since she and Blake look nothing at all alike. "I'm Margret." She grins before moving her eyes to Tanner. "My brother just left before you came in. He was on a roll about your new girlfriend."

"Margret," Tanner sighs.

"Hey." She holds up her hand. "I'm on your side with this one. I'm happy to see you're interested in something other than work. Hopefully, you'll rub off on my idiot brother, and he'll realize there's more to life than the lodge and making money." She shakes her head.

"I wouldn't count on that happening anytime soon. He married that place the day we signed the lease," Tanner says, and I squeeze his thigh when I catch a hint of disappointment in his tone.

"Well, I can hope, right?" She looks at me. "Sorry, Cybil, I'm sure you don't want to listen to me complain about my brother."

"It's okay. I get it."

"You have any siblings?"

"No, but my best friend is like my sister, and I could complain about her all day," I reply, and she laughs while Tanner chuckles.

"Right, well, enough about that. What are you two eating this fine morning?" she asks, and Tanner and I both rattle off our orders, and when we finish, she wanders off with a promise to return shortly with our coffees.

"I like her," I say, watching her stop at the table of an older couple on the way to the kitchen.

"She's easy to like, but you'll find out that Blake's whole family is like that, just good-to-the-core people."

"You're close with them all?"

"None of them gave me much of a choice. They brought me into the fold and wouldn't let me go."

"I love that for you," I tell him honestly. Without Jade and her parents, I don't know what would have happened to me, and even though he left his family by choice while mine was taken from me, I know how important it is to have people you can count on when things are difficult.

"Thanks, sunshine," he says quietly, leaning in to kiss me swiftly.

"So tell me," I prompt quietly, holding his gaze. "Do you always draw this much attention when you come to town? Because it feels like everyone in this place has been staring at us ever since we walked in the door."

"It's not me who's captured everyone's attention. I'm just sitting next to you."

"Right." I roll my eyes, and his hand comes up to capture my cheek and my attention.

"You're the most beautiful woman I've ever seen, Cybil, and that's not some line; it's the God's honest truth," he says, and I lick my lips as my cheeks warm. Not sure how to reply, because "Thank you" seems stupid and crying seems like a little bit of an overreaction, I bite my bottom lip. "It's also cute that you blush when I give you a compliment."

"It was a really nice compliment," I say quietly.

"It's just the truth," he replies just as quietly, holding my gaze.

"Tanner!" a deep voice calls, breaking into our moment, and he pulls out of the bubble we've found ourselves in. When I look to the side of the table and at the man standing there, I realize it's the bartender from the bar I ate at the first night I was in town. "I thought that was you."

"Mason." Tanner turns slightly to me. "You remember Cybil."

"I do." He gives me a wink and a smile, and I can't help but wonder how many women swoon when he turns his attention their way.

"Are you having breakfast?" Tanner asks.

"That was the plan, but the tables filled up, so I'm getting something to go."

"You should eat with us," I offer, motioning to the empty seats across from us.

"Oh, I don't—" he starts, shaking his head.

"Cybil's right. Join us," Tanner says, cutting him off.

"All right." He takes a seat and motions between us. "So how did this happen? The last time I saw you two in the same space, Cybil didn't seem to like you much."

"I spent a week convincing her that I wasn't a thief," Tanner says, and I laugh while elbowing him in the ribs.

"I'm sure there's a story there." Mason smiles; then his eyes move over Tanner's shoulder, and something in the look he has on his face has me turning to see what's captured his attention. When I see Margret with her head back, laughing at something, I turn back to Mason and notice his jaw clenching.

"So, Mason, have you known Tanner long?" I ask, and he blinks as he focuses on me.

"Since he started coming to town years ago."

"Mason and Blake grew up together," Tanner tells me.

"That's cool. This town is starting to feel like where I grew up, everyone knowing everyone."

"Small towns tend to be like that," Mason says. "How long are you in town for?"

"Six more days." I chew the inside of my cheek as the reminder makes my skin itch.

"Are you really going to be the third wheel on Tanner's first-ever date with a woman?" Margret breaks into the moment as she stops at the side of the table to pass Tanner and me the coffees she's holding.

"Yep." Mason shrugs; then his eyes drop to her stomach. "How's Little Miss Orange doing today?"

"She graduated. She's now the size of a grapefruit," she tells him, resting her hand on her stomach.

"Just three months left."

"I know." She blows out a long breath. "And I still have to take that birthing class."

"Is Hank going with you?" Mason asks, and Tanner's muscle tightens under my palm.

"I don't know—maybe, maybe not."

"I'll go if he doesn't show," he tells her, and I wonder who Hank is and why the air around us seems to have thickened with tension.

"Mason." She shakes her head.

"If he bails, I'm taking you, Margret." His tone brooks no argument, and she nods before looking over her shoulder when his name is called.

"Your to-go order is ready. Do you want me to change it to stay?"

"Nah." He pushes up to stand. "I have some stuff to take care of." He leans down and places a kiss on her cheek that causes her face to turn a pretty shade of pink; then he looks at Tanner and me. "Come to the bar for a drink before you head out of town."

"Sure." I nod before saying goodbye and turning to watch Margret and him chat near the door.

"Never gonna happen," Tanner says quietly, and I turn my head to meet his gaze.

"Pardon?"

"Margret and Mason are never gonna happen."

"Oh." My heart sinks. "They like each other, though, don't they?"

"Yeah."

"Well, you never know what might happen."

"I wouldn't get my hopes up about that situation, sunshine. He's one of Blake's best friends, so he won't go there, and she's still fucked up over her ex and praying he pulls his head out of his ass before their daughter comes screaming into the world."

"Her ex is a jerk?"

"Her ex is a dick," he says, and my nose scrunches.

"So how was everything?" Margret asks when we stop to pay at the register near the front door after eating.

"Delicious." I don't even hesitate to answer. Like Tanner promised, the coffee was a whole lot better than at the place down the street, and I don't even think I paused to take a breath between bites of pancakes because they were so good.

"So you'll be back." She grins at me, then looks at Tanner. "Mom said you two are coming to dinner this week."

"That's the plan."

"Good." She smiles at me. "And just so you know, Cybil, if you ever need a break from this Neanderthal, I'll give you my number. We can get lunch and putter around some of the shops down Main Street."

"I might just take you up on that. A few of the places we drove by on the way here looked cute, and I doubt Tanner would be fond of me dragging him around a dozen shops." I nudge his shoulder with mine.

"I'm going to have to veto you taking Cybil anywhere alone, since the last time you were out in town without supervision, you broke out the windows in Hank's truck and poured sugar in his gas tank."

"Wow, you really have no faith in me." She bats her lashes. "I'll have you know the cops said there wasn't proof that I had anything to do with that incident. Also, that entire situation could have been avoided if Hank was at work where he was supposed to be, instead of taking a woman out on a date."

"Right." Tanner sighs while I fight the urge to ask about a million and one questions. Like why the hell she is with Hank and not Mason, who is obviously into her, is clearly paying close attention to her pregnancy, and is willing to go with her to a birthing class.

"Anyway, enough about that." She locks eyes with me. "Ignore whatever he tells you about me when you two walk out the door, and"—her head dips after she rips off our receipt from the register and jots down her number, handing it to me—"use that if you need me to break you out of Tanner prison. I'll come help you escape."

"I'll call you." I can't help my grin as I tuck the piece of paper into the front pocket of my shorts.

"I knew I liked you." She grins back before turning her attention to a couple who walks through the door, causing the bell to ding. "Duty calls." She gives us a smile before grabbing two menus from the holder on the counter. As she walks around to greet them, we head out the door.

"I don't care what you say. I'm going to pray to whatever god is listening that Mason and Margret get together," I tell Tanner when he opens the door to let me into his truck.

"Why am I not surprised by that?"

"Because girls gotta stick together, and she and Mason are obviously perfect for each other."

"Cybil . . ." He starts to say more, but I cover my ears with my hands, then watch him shake his head before he shuts my door. When he gets in behind the wheel a moment later, he raises a brow, and I remove my hands. "All right, sunshine, where to now?"

"I'm okay with whatever we do, but I do need to stop by the store to get some body wash and stuff, since I don't have much, and whatever that bar soap is you have in the shower isn't going to work for me."

"Are you going to fill my shower with girly shit?" he questions, reaching over to wrap his hand around the back of my neck and pull me closer.

"Yes, do you have an issue with that?" I ask, slightly breathless, and his eyes scan my face as he seems to ponder the question.

"Not even a little bit."

"Good," I say, not having much time to think about the fact that my heart suddenly feels a little too big for my chest as he leans in, covering my mouth with his. As his tongue slides across mine, my thighs press tightly together. I wish we weren't in his truck.

Or at least not in his truck in a public space outside a busy restaurant.

Chapter 17

Tanner

With Cybil lying on top of me—the softness of her curves pressed against me from chest to thigh—and my eyes to the TV, I settle in the feeling of contentment that only she seems to be able to give me.

"Later on, will you help me wrap my hand for a shower? I did it this morning, but some water got in, so I'm obviously not as good as you are," she says, and I tip my head down as she places her chin on the back of her hand that's resting against my chest.

"Sure." I push her hair back away from her pretty face as her fingers move to my bottom lip. Looking into her eyes, I think back to her comment yesterday about this being so easy. She's right; this shit between us is easy, from conversation to just being like we are right now, lying out on the couch in the living room, watching a movie. Every moment feels like we've done it all before, even though we haven't, not with each other.

I keep waiting for her to do or say something that will annoy me, or for me to do or say something that annoys her, but it hasn't happened since we met, which makes me wonder if it will. Then again, real life hasn't touched us much since we got off the mountain, so only time will tell.

"What are you thinking about?" she asks, moving up to straddle my waist, and my cock jerks against my zipper.

"How perfect you are." I grab hold of her hips to hold her steady.

"I'm not perfect." Her hands move to rest against my chest. "Far from it."

"Hmmm." I move my hand under her shirt and slide it up her side, feeling her shiver as my fingers smooth over her soft skin. "From where I'm sitting, you're perfect." I cup her breast, and her head falls back to her shoulders before she dips down and locks her gaze with mine, the look in her eyes making my dick throb.

"Please don't tease me, Tanner."

"Tease you?" I smile, and she frowns at my mouth. "Sunshine, when have I teased you?"

"Since the first time you kissed me you've been teasing me." Her breath hitches as my thumb scrapes across her nipple through the lace of her bra, and my other hand slides into her hair so I can drag her mouth closer. "Last night, you definitely teased me."

"Last night, I didn't want you to hurt yourself." I lift up to kiss the pout off her lips. "I still don't want you to hurt yourself."

"I won't hurt myself, but I might hurt you if you don't take things past second base," she says, trying to sound stern, and I chuckle. "I'm not joking, Tanner."

"I see that, sunshine." I sit up, adjusting her in my hold. "But there's no need to get violent." I listen to her laugh right before I whip her shirt off over her head and lower my mouth to her breasts that I've captured in my palms. I kiss up her neck, and she lets out a squeak as I move my hands to her ass and stand.

"Tanner," she moans against my lips as I start down the hall with her in my arms, and having her mouth on mine makes it almost impossible to walk in a straight line. Then her body freezes, and my footsteps pause when there's a loud knock on the front door.

"No." I drop my forehead to hers.

"Were you expecting anyone?" Her whispered pant has my fingers flexing into the cheeks of her ass, still in my hands.

"No, it's probably just a package being dropped off or something." I start to move us toward the bedroom, then curse when the doorbell rings.

"You should make sure it's not something important." She wiggles to get down, but I don't let her go. I drop my eyes to her swollen lips, her hair spilling over her shoulder, and her breasts, still heaving. "Tanner." She grabs my face. "Let me go, and answer the door."

"All right, but I'll meet you in bed as soon as I get rid of whoever's at the door." I set her on her feet, and she nods before turning for the room while I head for the door, pretty sure I'm going to kill someone when the bell goes off again.

When I reach the entryway, my brows drag together. Standing outside the glass door on my front porch are Margret and her best friend, Cammy, along with Mav, Blake, and Mason. As I get closer, Margret spots me and starts to wave wildly while Cammy shakes her head at her. I pull open the door and start to ask what the fuck is going on but don't get the chance.

"We brought dinner." Margret lifts a small shopping bag before walking past me into the house.

"Sorry, Tanner," Cammy says quietly as she follows Margret, and I move my gaze to the men still standing outside.

"Margret insisted we bring dinner to make Cybil feel welcome," Blake grumbles, not looking happy about the idea, while Mav and Mason share a look.

"Did you think to tell her no?" I ask, crossing my arms over my chest and glaring at the three of them.

"We all tried, but she couldn't be stopped," Mason says, walking past me with Blake following him.

"A phone call would have been appreciated," I tell Mav, and he shrugs while trying to hide his smile. "Payback is a motherfucker. You know that, right?"

"Don't be pissed at me. Besides, Margret just wanted—and I quote—'Blake to see how happy and cute you and Cybil are together.'"

"Great," I mutter before closing the door behind him and locking it. When we hit the kitchen, I notice the girls are both unpacking the bags they brought in, while Blake and Mason are opening beers. "Give me five."

I walk past them and head for the bedroom. When I don't see Cybil in the room, I go to the bathroom and find her coming out of the closet wearing a new shirt, this one a thin white material that's hanging off one shoulder with about a thousand holes cut in the material.

"I heard voices, so I figured I should get dressed." She closes the distance between us and rests her hands on my chest. "Is everything okay?"

"Besides the fact that Margret, her friend Cammy, Mav, Blake, and Mason showed up with dinner when I had a whole different set of plans for us tonight, yeah, it's all good." I wrap my hand around her hip as she laughs. "Do you think that's funny?"

"No, just thinking this is a little payback for teasing me last night."

"Is that so?" I lean down and nip her bottom lip while my hand slides into the back of her jean shorts, and my fingers find the wetness between her legs, making her jump. "You're wet, babe."

"Tanner."

"Yeah, sunshine?" I slide my fingers back and forth over her sex, keeping my strokes gentle.

"I think I might hate you right now." She gets up on her tiptoes, bringing her mouth closer to mine, and bites my bottom lip hard enough to sting.

"That wasn't very nice." I move my hand to the front of her shorts and find her clit with ease. "Put your hand on my shoulder and leave it there, or I stop."

"Oh God." Her head falls back, and her hips buck as she rests her wrist on my shoulder.

"And you gotta be quiet, sunshine."

"If you stop when I'm so clos—"

"I won't stop unless you move your hand," I say, interrupting her threat, and her eyes open to meet mine, then widen in shock—or maybe it's awe—when I circle her entrance and her clit. I know the instant she starts to come. Her pupils dilate, her mouth opens on a gasp, and her pussy starts to clench. Hearing her whimper and feeling the nails of her good hand dig into my biceps, I cover her mouth with mine and swallow down her moan before slowly easing my hand from between her legs. When really, I want nothing more than to slide her shorts down her hips, wrap her legs around my waist, and plunge into her.

"Don't let me go," she whispers when I drag my mouth from hers and remove my hand from her pants.

"I won't." I smile at the satisfied look on her face. "Still hate me?"

"Not anymore." She laughs, dropping her forehead to my chest, where she whispers, "Thank you."

"I'm here for that anytime you need me." I kiss the top of her head while my arms wrap around her.

"I think I can stand without the risk of falling on my face now."

"You sure?"

"Yeah." She lifts her head, putting her hand to my cheek to run her thumb over my lip where she bit me. "Sorry about that."

"I'm not complaining." I kiss the tip of her nose, watching her face soften.

"We should probably get out to your friends before they think we're being rude."

"Since they showed up uninvited, they can stay out there all night by themselves for all I care."

"Now, that would be rude." She grins before leaning up to place a kiss on my jaw and then steps away from me. "I'm just . . . umm . . . I'll be right back." She hurries to the small room where the toilet is and closes the door, while I go to the sink to wash my hands and will my cock to die down as I adjust my erection. After she comes out and washes her hands, we leave the room together and head to the kitchen, where Margret and Cammy are cutting up vegetables and the guys are nowhere in sight.

"Cybil." Margret smiles when she spots us. "This is my best friend, Cammy. Cammy, this is Cybil."

"Nice to meet you." Cybil gives her a wave, then looks around. "Do you need help with anything?"

"You can be in charge of skewering the veggies for the kabobs." Margret passes Cybil a pack of sticks, then looks at me. "The guys are out starting the grill. I don't know why three of them need to start it or why they haven't come back in. Maybe they need you to go out there to sing 'Kumbaya' while holding hands."

"I'll go help them." I hook Cybil around the side of her neck, and she looks at me. "Are you okay in here with these two?"

"She's fine." Margret laughs and Cybil glances at her, smiling before meeting my gaze once more.

"I'm good. Go hang with the guys."

"Wait." Margret holds out a beer toward me. "I think you'll need this for your fire-starting ritual."

"Thanks." I take it and kiss the side of Cybil's head before I leave out the back door.

When I step outside, Mav turns my way. "Leave it to you to purchase the most fucking complicated barbecue around."

"It's not complicated. You just gotta know how to use it." I flip up the switch on the wall that's attached to the gas hidden under the deck. "Now turn the knob."

He does, and the middle row of flames comes to life, followed by the others.

"Well, that was easy," Mason mumbles before taking a swig of his beer.

I twist the top off mine, flicking the piece of metal toward the garbage in the corner, then look at Blake, noticing the annoyed look on his face. "You still pissed about Cybil and me?"

"No." His gaze meets mine.

"Then what crawled up your ass?"

"Margret told him that Cammy's boyfriend is going to propose," Mason says, and Blake shoots a glare his way, and he holds up his hand. "Just saying, I know that's what's had you in a shit mood all day."

"I couldn't give one fuck about Cammy marrying some douchebag banker from Missoula."

"Right," Mav mumbles into his beer before tipping it back, and I do the same with mine, knowing it's pointless to even broach the subject of feelings and emotions with Blake. He would rather pull out his nails one by one than admit he's jealous, which I know he is.

Cammy is probably the only woman who could ever take his attention away from work, and I'm guessing that's the problem. The issue with that is that she's pretty, educated, and too smart to wait for him to realize there's more to life than making money. Case in point—her man getting ready to put a ring on her finger.

"When is Cybil heading home?" Mav asks, and even knowing the question is meant to change the subject, my jaw clenches on the word *home*, and my chest feels funny at the mention of her leaving. Two things that don't bode well for me when the time does come for her to go back to Oregon.

"We haven't talked about it."

"We have a new set of clients coming in next week." Blake takes a seat on one of the folding lawn chairs stacked against the wall. "Mav is scheduled to take them out, so I'll need you to help me with the runs and office shit."

"Do you think I somehow forgot how shit has gone for the last two years and suddenly need you to remind me of what my job is?"

"You've been distracted, so maybe."

"Christ, Mason's right. You are in a shit mood. But you know me, brother, and you know I'm not the one. You wanna act like a dick, then you can take that shit somewhere else. That or you can grow a pair and actually deal with whatever it is that's got you fucked up," I say, and his teeth grind.

He opens his mouth like he's going to say something, but then he shuts it, and I know why a second later when the door behind me opens and the girls come out.

"I really hope you four were able to start the grill, because I'm starving," Margret says, then stops and looks around. "What happened, and why do you two look ready to kill each other?" She motions between Blake and me.

"Guy stuff," Mason says as he takes the tray Cammy's carrying and places it next to the barbecue.

"Well, cheer up," she orders, "because I can't drink myself into a state of 'I don't give a fuck,' and I really have no desire to spend the night watching you two glare at each other." Mason laughs while Cybil drops a plate with steaks on it next to the grill before she comes over and tucks herself under my arm.

"We're all good," Blake tells her, getting up from the chair he was in and motioning for her to sit. "And you really do need to stop cursing so much all the time."

"Don't even start on that again." Margret rolls her eyes at him as she falls into his seat, rubbing her belly. "I don't curse that much, and the little miss can't make out anything I say right now."

"You curse more than your brother," Mav tells her, and she flips him the bird. He grins at her, shaking his head.

"The problem is I shouldn't have let you hang with me and my friends all the time when we were kids," Blake mutters while unfolding a few more chairs.

"They weren't your friends; they were mine." She smirks at him. "Or at least they all liked me more than they liked you."

"Smart-ass." He smiles for the first time since he got here, which makes me relax slightly.

"Someone's phone is ringing," Cammy says, and Cybil looks up at me.

"I think that's me. I'll be right back."

Once she's inside, I take a seat in one of the chairs and raise a brow at Margret when I find her watching me. "What?"

"I love her, like . . . *love her*, love her. You'd better not mess this up."

"I wasn't planning on it," I say as the door behind me opens, and I turn to watch Cybil come out. "Everything okay?"

"Yeah, it was the girl who runs my website. She just wanted to give me a heads-up about a glitch on my site that might mean I receive some weird emails until she gets it sorted."

"Got it." I drag her down to sit on my lap, and instead of trying to move, she gets comfortable. As the mood lightens and everyone including her falls into the ease there's always been with our group, I hold her a little tighter, wondering how the fuck I'm going to be able to let her go and starting to doubt I'll be able to at all.

Chapter 18

Cybil

I stand under Tanner's arm and wave as Mav, Blake, Cammy, Margret, and Mason head off down the lane. It was a great night, even with the ever-present undercurrent of tension that seemed to fill the air. As Tanner leads me back into the house and shuts the door, I open my mouth to tell him that I like his friends but end up squeaking when he turns me to face him and presses me against the wall in the entryway.

"Time to finish what we started earlier." He grins at me before dropping his mouth down to mine. I don't hesitate to kiss him back; then it's a race to get each other undressed as we make out, our hands roaming over each other as we pass the living room and kitchen and head down the hall. When we reach the bedroom, Tanner pushes me back onto the bed, where I land with a bounce.

"Hand above your head, sunshine, and don't move it," he orders, and I instantly comply as he crawls up the bed and kneels between my legs. Startling me, he spreads my legs wide, then uses his fingers to hold me open and ducks his head to suck on my clit. Never having experienced anything like this in my life, I don't know if I should push him away or beg him to never stop. But as the sensation of bliss hits me, I hold on to his hair with one hand, making sure to keep my damaged hand above my head where he told me to keep it, not wanting to give him any reason to stop what he's doing. A task that is almost impossible as my toes curl and my insides turn liquid.

"Tanner." His name comes out on a moan as his tongue circles my clit and his fingers pump in and out of me in a rhythm that is maddening. As I lift my hips to get closer, to get more, my head bows off the bed and my core begins to clench. I thought I knew what an orgasm was, but standing in his bathroom earlier, he showed me I was wrong, and now he's proving that what I felt earlier wasn't some kind of fluke: a buildup of sexual frustration that meant I came harder than I ever had before within minutes, if not seconds, of him touching me.

"Oh God," I whimper as his lips wrap around my clit and he sucks. Tapping that hidden spot, he sends me into a tailspin. My breath catches, stars start to dance behind my closed eyelids, and my body seems to vibrate from the inside out. Dizzy and panting for breath, I fall flat on the bed and cover my face with my hands as I fight the urge to laugh and cry at the same time.

"You did good, sunshine." I feel his smile against my belly button before his lips trail up my stomach, then between my breasts. When his knee bumps my legs farther apart and he makes room for himself between my thighs, I remove my hands and stare into his beautiful eyes that are dark with lust and warm with some emotion that makes me feel hot all over. "Cybil."

"Yeah?" I place my hand on his bare shoulder, lift my leg up over his hip, and use it to pull him closer.

"You okay?" he asks gruffly, sweeping my hair off my forehead.

"Better than okay," I admit truthfully. I don't think I've ever been happier than I am right now. I don't think I've ever felt more connected to another person, and that should scare me, given how long we've known each other, but it doesn't freak me out. Not anymore. Now it just feels like this is how it's supposed to be.

"Are you okay?" My breath hitches when I feel the head of his cock bump against my entrance.

"I'm with you, your taste is on my tongue, you're naked in my bed, and it's too late for visitors. So, yeah, I'm good." He brushes his smiling lips across mine before he deepens the kiss and cups my breast, pinching my nipple and causing a zip of heat to spread between my legs.

Pulling my mouth from his, I reach between us and wrap my hand around his length. "I need you."

"You have me, all of me." He bends, which means I lose my hold on him but gain his mouth on my breast and his thumb on my clit. I thread my fingers through his hair, arch my back, and wrap my legs around his hips when he moves to my neglected breast. Not sure how much more I can take, not when I'm on edge once again, I tug his hair until he lets go, leaning up enough to place my mouth against his. But I only get it for a second before his hand reaches over to a drawer next to the bed and comes out a moment later with a condom.

As he leans back and rips the black packet open with his teeth, I trail my hand down his torso, fascinated by how he can be so smooth and hard everywhere at the same time. I watch in complete fascination as his muscles bunch under his smooth skin when he slides the condom down his length. When he has the condom on, his body forces mine back onto the bed, right before his hand wraps around my hip and his mouth catches mine. Lost in the weight of his body, the smell of his skin, and the deepness of his kiss, I whimper as his hand slides between us and dig my nails into his flesh as he begins to enter me in a smooth stroke. Full, so full, his body stills, and he pulls back just far enough to rest his forehead against mine while his eyes squeeze tight.

"Tanner." I wrap my hand around the side of his neck, and his eyes open as his ragged breath brushes my lips.

"Give me a minute, baby," he says, and I lift my hips, listening to him groan right before his fingers dig into my thigh. "I'm really trying not to lose myself, but you're hot, and tight, and *you*, which means if you move, there's no guarantee this won't be finished before it's even started."

"Sorry." I bite my bottom lip and will myself to stay still, not sure I'll be able to—not for very long, at least, and the fact that he wants me so much is making me powerful. I've never had anyone crave me the way he does, and it makes it all the more clear that what Galvin and I shared wasn't what it should have been. Thankfully, I don't have to wait long, because he pulls out slowly, then slides back in, the sensation causing the muscles in my lower belly to tighten and my core to pulse. It shouldn't be possible to orgasm from just this, from just having him inside me, but just like that, I'm close once again.

"Cybil." My name sounds like a curse right before his mouth crashes down on mine, and his tongue slips between my lips. I kiss him back, willing my body to keep from flying over the edge as his thrusts speed up, his hips pounding into mine.

My legs wrap around his waist, and I dig my fingers into his ribs as his mouth leaves mine and travels, nipping and licking down my neck until he reaches my breast, where he pulls my nipple into his mouth. He sucks hard, causing my core to tighten almost painfully as I fight off my orgasm.

"Let go, Cybil," he orders, and I shake my head, not ready to lose the feelings coursing through me—not yet, not when it feels like I've waited my whole life for this moment. "Yes." His hand slides between us, his teeth nipping my chin then bottom lip before he kisses me once more.

Completely overwhelmed, I let go without a choice and cry out his name while he growls mine, his hips jerking once, then twice, before he stills deep inside me. With my heart pounding and feeling his beating just as hard against my breast, I pant for breath and wrap my arms around him, accepting his weight as he collapses on top of me. Tears fill my eyes as my body continues to pulse, but I fight them back, not wanting to have to explain why I'm crying, when I don't even know.

"You know"—he pulls back after a moment and locks his gaze on mine—"I keep waiting for something, anything to show me that this—you and I—are not going to work, but I don't think it's going to happen," he says gently, making my stomach bottom out as his eyes roam my face. "We're gonna need to talk about what happens after you go back to Oregon." His fingers smooth down my jaw before they trace the lower edge of my lip. "Not right now." He covers my lips with his finger when I open my mouth to ask what he wants. "Not now, but before our time is up, we'll figure out what we're going to do. Because I'm going to want to see you for more than a week every few months. A whole lot more than that."

"Okay, we'll talk about it and figure it out." I move my hand to his chest, over his heart, wondering if his hurts like mine does right now at the thought of me leaving. I want to say I'd stay if he asked me to, but the truth is my whole life is somewhere else. My friends, family, and everything I've ever known are in Oregon, but I'm starting to see that there's more to life than my small town. And a good thing is I can work from anywhere, which makes this situation a little less complicated.

"How about a bath?" He runs his nose across mine.

"I don't think I've taken a bath since I was a kid," I say, and without a word, he slowly pulls out of me, then pushes off the bed and reaches out for my hand.

When we get into the bathroom, he lets me go just long enough to deal with the condom. Then he turns on the tub that looks like it could fit three people comfortably and dumps in a glob of something from a blue bottle under the faucet. As the smell of mint fills the room, he lifts me off my feet and places my naked bottom on the counter, making my breath hitch.

"Sorry, just wanna get you wrapped up." He takes my hand and deftly puts on one of the plastic gloves he stole from the hospital and tapes around my wrist. "All done." He lifts me down. "I'll be back."

When he leaves, I get into the bath and am covered under a layer of bubbles when he comes back holding something that makes me smile. "Are you going to read?" I motion to my book in his hand.

"Yep."

I somehow manage to keep my eyes on his face, even as he walks toward the tub; then I scoot forward when he motions me to, and he gets in behind me, placing his legs on the outside of mine.

"Good?" he asks, wrapping his arm across my upper chest, urging me to lean back against him.

"Yeah," I reply, and he opens the book to the page he left off on. As he reads, I close my eyes and relax against him completely, the sound of his voice and the hot water washing away the stress of today.

"Cybil," he calls after a long while, and I turn to look at him over my shoulder.

"Yeah?"

"I thought you fell asleep." He sets the book down on the side of the tub.

"Just relaxed." I roll so I'm resting on my stomach, which places his rock-hard cock right between my breasts.

"Come here." He drags me up his body until I'm straddling him. "How's your hand?" he asks—or I'm pretty sure that's what he asked. It's hard to tell with the sound of my heart pumping in my ears as the feel of him between my legs makes me dizzy.

"Fine," I breathe as he leans up and bites my earlobe before dragging it through his teeth, causing me to roll my hips in response. As his hand latches around my waist, I reach between us, and the moment he's in position, I don't hesitate, sinking down onto his length. "Yesss." I drop my forehead to rest against his. Not only is he thick, but he's also long, making me feel impossibly full in this position.

"Are you okay?" The question is strained.

"Yes." I nod, and both his hands move to my waist so he can lift me up and urge me back down. As he picks up speed and I fall into sync with him, water sloshes over the side of the tub. I lean back, and as one of his hands moves to cup my breast, the look on his face almost sends me over the edge. I didn't grow up questioning my appearance, but I've never had anyone look at me the way he does.

"Fuck, you really are perfect, sunshine. So fucking beautiful." He urges me down harder. "Touch yourself." Slowly, I move my hand over my breast, then down my stomach and between my legs. The moment I circle my clit that is still sensitive from my earlier orgasms, my inner walls tighten, and he curses, "Don't fucking stop."

"Tanner."

"I'm right here, baby." His hand around my hip urges me to move faster and harder, which sends him deeper and deeper; then his mouth latches onto my breast.

When his tongue lashes against my nipple and his teeth nip the sensitive flesh, blinding white heat spreads through my body and my core in spasms, sending me closer to the edge. Lost in the sensation of him, heat begins to pool in my lower belly, and I know I won't be able to hold off for long. It's too much; it's all too much.

"Let go, sunshine." He drags my mouth down to his, and his tongue thrusts between my lips. The taste of him sinks into my senses, and I lose the ability to hold back, no matter how much I don't want this to end. I fall over the edge, whimpering his name as I shove my face into his neck and hold on to him with every piece of me, feeling him jerk and his grip on me tighten.

"I don't think I'm going to be able to let you go."

His softly spoken confession has the tears I felt earlier crawling up my throat, only this time, I don't fight them. I let them go as I give him a piece of my heart he doesn't even know he has.

Sitting on the back deck, with the morning sun sparkling through the trees and the sound of nature alive in the forest just outside the screened-in porch, I take a sip of coffee as I watch Tanner do push-ups.

"Do you work out every day?" I tuck my feet under me and pull down his T-shirt I stole from him, so at least my ass is covered.

"Most days."

"I should work out with you," I say absently, watching his elbows bend and his biceps flex.

"I wouldn't mind giving you a workout." He stops with his arms straight in a plank position and moves his eyes over my bare legs, my breasts, and face, the heat in his look causing my nipples to pebble and wetness to spread between my legs. Really, it should be impossible for me to be turned on after the night and morning we had, but there you go. One look and a few words from him and I'm ready all over again. After experiencing sex with Tanner, I now know what I was missing; sex with Galvin was routine at best, probably because he wasn't into it and I had no idea what I was doing or what I was missing out on.

"Don't turn me on when I need sustenance."

"I'll feed you after I work out." He gives me a grin before he goes back to doing push-ups. "Then I'll eat you after we have breakfast."

"You're so bad." I laugh, leaning forward to grab my cell phone when it starts to ring. When I see it's Galvin calling, I hit the ignore button. I've said everything I need to say to him, and I'm not at a place where we can be friends. When it starts to ring again almost immediately, I frown and set down my coffee, then pick my cell up, slide my finger across the screen, and put it to my ear. "Yes?"

"Cybil." His voice sounds weird, worried, strained.

"What happened?" I sit up as my heart starts to pound. "Is Jade okay?"

"Jade's fine, but she asked me to call you. We were on the phone this morning, and her mom started to complain about her chest hurting before she passed out. They're on the way to the hospital. They think she had a heart attack."

A sense of dread washes over me while the blood in my head seems to rush to my toes, making me lightheaded.

"I . . ." Tears fill my eyes as I realize I'm not just minutes away, but hundreds of miles, which means I can't just get in my Bronco to go be with my best friend who needs me. "Oh God." I cover my mouth with my fingers.

"Cybil," Galvin calls, but before I can respond, my phone slides from my hand and Tanner places his fingers under my chin, scanning my face. He moves his hand to the back of my head and presses my forehead into his hip.

"This is Tanner. What's going on?" he asks; then his fingers dig into my scalp. "Now is not the time for that conversation. Cybil's upset, and I wanna know why." The sound of my heart beating hard fills my ears, then his rumbled, "What hospital? All right, let Jade know we're on our way." I hear my cell bounce onto the cushion of the couch, then land on the floor before he gets down on his knees in front of me and takes my face into his hands. "Sunshine, I know you're upset, but I need you to keep it together."

"Maisie's in the hospital."

"I know." His expression softens as he wipes the tears from my cheeks.

"I'm hundreds of miles away." My chin wobbles. "And Jade needs me."

"You'll be with her, baby." He stands and pulls me up, then urges me into the house and to the bedroom. At the side of the bed, he turns me to face him and wraps his hand around my jaw. "Get dressed and pack what you need to pack. I'm gonna make a couple of calls." He kisses my nose, then turns to leave.

I blink at the empty doorway, then look around the room before I get myself together enough to put on some clothes and to start packing up my stuff. As I'm shoving my makeup bag in my suitcase, he comes into the room and walks past me to go into the bathroom without a word; then I hear the shower turn on. As I finish packing, I try to figure out how I'll be able to drive, especially with the tears I'm barely holding back, ready to let loose at any second.

"Are you packed?" he asks a few minutes later as he comes out of the bathroom fully dressed. Wearing sneakers, jeans, and a T-shirt, with a backward baseball cap on his head, he has a black duffle bag slung over his shoulder. If things were different, I would take a moment to appreciate how good he looks wearing a baseball cap, but now isn't the time.

"Yeah." I flip my suitcase closed, and he moves me out of the way to zip it up for me.

"Blake's dad is meeting us at the airport in Missoula in the next hour, so we need to get on the road."

"What?" I watch as he lifts my bag off the bed.

"He's going to fly us to Portland, and Janet called a rental-car place at the airport there, so we'll have wheels when we land."

Shaking my head, I try to wrap my head around what he's saying. "Are you coming with me?"

"Yes." He places his hand against my lower back and urges me out of the room.

"You're coming with me, and Blake's dad is flying us . . . like, in a plane?"

"Unless he decides to take out the dragons, yeah, he's flying us in his plane," he says, and I stop and turn to face him. "Sorry, shit, baby. I didn't mean—"

"I've never flown in my life," I admit, cutting him off. "I've never even been near a plane. I don't think—"

"It's safe, Cybil, and the most logical way for us to get to Oregon."

"I watch the news. I—"

"You"—he captures the back of my neck and smooths his thumb up and down my skin—"trust me."

"I trust you." I don't even hesitate to agree, and he places his face close to mine, so close I can see tiny bits of gold in his eyes I didn't notice before, something that's ridiculous to notice now.

"This is the fastest way to get you home to your family. I promise you'll be safe. I'll be with you the entire time, so you have nothing to be afraid of. Okay?" Swallowing, I nod, and he leans in to kiss the tip of my nose. "You need to grab your cell from the back deck while I make sure the house is shut down."

"Okay." I head outside to get my phone while he goes to the kitchen, and when I get back inside, he ushers me to the front door and out, leading me to his truck. While I buckle up, I hear the thud of our bags landing in the truck bed; then, a moment later, he gets in behind the wheel.

"Ready?" he asks, placing two bottled waters in the cup holders and a few of my favorite granola bars in the center console between our seats. The sight of them causes my throat to burn as I nod. "Let's get you home." He grabs my hand and pulls it over to rest on his thigh before he starts the engine and backs away from the house. As he flips on the turn signal and turns onto the main road, I look at my phone, hoping it will ring while praying it doesn't. I don't know what I'll do if I get a call saying that—

I bite the inside of my cheek, refusing to finish my thought.

"I'm proud of you, baby."

"You always say you're proud of me when I'm not doing anything worthy of that praise." I smile, but it feels forced.

"You're doing more than you think you are. I know you're freaked, but you're not breaking down on me." He gives my fingers a squeeze, and I look over at him. "You should send Jade a message to let her know you're on your way and that you'll be there in less than four hours."

"Four hours?" There's no hiding the surprise in my voice.

"It's about an hour-and-a-half flight once we're wheels up, then a forty-minute drive from the airport to the hospital." He lifts my hand to kiss my fingers. "After you send that text, I want you to eat one of your granola bars."

"I'm not hungry."

"I know, but you need to get something in your stomach. It's going to be a long day," he says gently, and I nod before quickly sending Jade a message and another to Galvin. Jade doesn't respond, but Galvin texts back seconds later, saying he's in the waiting room at the hospital and that he'll see me when I get there. Which I'm not looking forward to. I don't text him back.

I grab one of my bars and go through the motions of chewing and swallowing, because Tanner is right. I'll need something in my stomach if I'm going to face this day.

Chapter 19

Tanner

I grab the parking pass the machine spits out, then wait for the gate to go up before heading up the ramp into the parking garage across the street from the hospital. When we landed an hour ago, Cybil was able to get ahold of Jade. She told her that Maisie had gone in for emergency surgery after the doctors had confirmed she did have a heart attack and that she needed a stent put in.

After getting that news, Cybil assured her that she was on her way before hanging up and breaking into tears that ripped me apart as they soaked my tee. It took me a good ten minutes to get her calm enough to get off the plane. Dave looked about as happy as I felt seeing her cry, which meant she'd won him over just as quickly as she has everyone else in my life.

Finally finding an empty space on the third level, I pull in and park, then give Cybil's thigh a squeeze.

"You okay, sunshine?" I move my hand to the back of her neck under her ponytail, and she turns my way.

"I hate hospitals," she says quietly, and my fingers automatically tighten on her nape. Her confession isn't surprising. I imagine that after her mom was diagnosed with cancer, she probably spent more time in hospitals than she ever wanted to.

"That's understandable," I assure her, and her chin trembles. Hating that there's nothing I can do to ease her fear right now, I pull her close and rest my forehead against hers. "It will be okay, even if it doesn't feel like it will be."

"Don't make me cry." She pulls in a deep breath and lets it out slowly. "Not when I need to be strong for Jade."

"Sunshine, Jade is going to understand you being upset." I kiss her nose, then lean back. "Are you ready to go inside?" With a nod, she grabs her purse, and I get out, then meet her at her door. It takes a few minutes once we get inside the hospital to find the waiting room outside surgery, but as soon as we arrive, Cybil lets go of my hand and rushes right for a redhead with long hair. She's being held by a burly older gentleman with hair as white as snow and a beard that hasn't been trimmed since the seventies. When the two of them spot Cybil, they wrap her in an embrace and start to rock her back and forth.

Not wanting to interrupt, I stand back with my arms crossed over my chest, giving them a moment. As they start to talk in hushed tones, I notice two men standing a couple of feet away and know exactly who they are without an introduction. If I had to guess, the tall blond with short hair and classic all-American features, dressed like he belongs in Montana on a ranch, is her ex, Galvin. The bald guy with glasses at his side, who's dressed like he was out running, in shorts, sneakers, and a plain shirt, is her ex's new husband, Chris.

As I study the two of them, the sour expression on Chris's face as he stares at Cybil begins to piss me off. I'm sure he's angry that the guy he's now married to was in a relationship with someone else while in a relationship with him, but that shit has nothing to do with Cybil. If anyone has the right to feel victimized, it's her, since she's the only one who was left in the dark. When I see Galvin move to make his presence known, I drop my arms to my sides and step toward Cybil, which draws his attention to me. He stops, his eyes widening. Not giving a fuck what he's thinking, I place my hand against Cybil's lower back once I'm close enough to touch her, and she tips her head back toward me, giving me a sad but somewhat relieved smile.

"Jade just told me that right before we got here, the doctors came down to let them know Maisie is out of surgery and stable. They're putting her in a room now."

"That's great news, sunshine."

"Yeah." She reaches for my hand and laces her fingers with mine before introducing me to Jade and her father by lifting our hands and stating, "Jade, Bernard, this is Tanner. Tanner, this is my family."

"Nice to meet you both." I dip my chin.

"I wish it were under better circumstances." Bernard holds his hand out toward me, and the moment I take it, he pulls me forward to pound my bicep, saying quietly, "Thank you for getting Cybil here so quickly."

"Anytime," I reply, and he lets me go, looking away, but not before I catch the torment he's trying to hide.

"Tanner." Jade gives me a somber smile while reaching out to give my hand a squeeze. "It's nice to meet you."

"You too," I say, and Cybil rests against me, so I wrap my arm around her waist and tuck her into my side.

"Cybil." As soon as the man I noticed earlier says her name, her body against mine grows rigid, and she turns his way.

"Galvin, Chris," she says, the tone of her voice not exactly cold, but neither is it welcoming. "Thank you for calling me to let me know about Maisie."

"Yeah." Galvin's gaze pings between Cybil and me. "Do you think we can talk?" He swallows hard, and his husband's jaw twitches, making me wonder what Galvin's told him about Cybil's and his relationship.

"I'm thinking right now isn't the time for that," I cut in before she can answer, not giving a fuck if I'm overstepping.

"Tanner's right," Bernard rumbles, narrowing his gaze on Galvin. "You wanna talk to Cybil, you do it another time, not right now when the woman who helped raise her is in a hospital bed."

"Of course." Galvin shakes his head. "I just—"

"You're just thinking about yourself," Bernard says, cutting his gaze to Chris before giving Galvin another look that has his shoulders sagging.

"We should go," Chris inserts, wrapping his hand around Galvin's bicep.

"Yeah, okay." Galvin looks at Cybil quickly before focusing on Jade. "Will you call and let me know when your mom can have visitors?"

"Of course," Jade says, giving him a hug; then she looks between him and Chris. "Thanks for coming."

"If you need anything, let us know," he tells her, sending Cybil one more long glance before Chris takes his hand and urges him out of the waiting room.

"You know, Dad, you could be a little nicer to him." Jade sighs, wrapping her arms around his middle when he places his arm around her shoulders.

"I didn't kick his ass. I consider that pretty nice," Bernard grumbles, and I bite back a smile while Jade hisses.

"Dad."

"Don't 'Dad' me. He hurt Cybil. God only knows how long he knew he wanted to be with someone else." He shakes his head, then looks past Cybil and me.

I turn to look over my shoulder and find an older woman in scrubs walking toward us. When she's close, she looks us over before she locks eyes with Bernard. "Maisie is settled in her room. You can stay with her overnight if you like, of course, but there can only be two people in the room at a time. Visitors can only stay for fifteen minutes until she's moved out of the ICU, which won't be until tomorrow, and visiting hours are up at eight."

"Thanks, Annie," Bernard says, and she pats his arm before she turns to Cybil.

"It's good to see you back, kid."

"You too, Annie," Cybil replies, and Annie glances up at me quickly, then gives Cybil a soft smile, walking away.

"All right." Bernard drops his arm from Jade's shoulders. "You and Cybil go on up and see your mom."

"No, you and Jade go first," Cybil says quickly, shaking her head.

"I'm gonna be here all night, and Maisie will want to see her girls," he says gruffly, and Jade's eyes fill with tears while Cybil tucks her face against my side and sniffles.

"Go on with Jade." I rub her back, then kiss the top of her head, and she nods before tipping her head back, her gaze searching mine. "I'll be here when you get back."

With a nod, she looks at Jade, then reaches for her hand, and the two of them walk away.

"I need coffee." Bernard rubs his hands down his face.

"We passed the cafeteria on the way up here. The coffee shop there was open. I can run and get you something."

"Do you think they have whiskey?"

"That's doubtful." I smile, and he sighs.

"I probably shouldn't drink anyway." He pats my back. "I need a break from this room, so I'll wander with you down to the cafeteria."

Without another word, we head down the hall to the coffee shop, and while he gets a coffee, I pull out my cell phone when it vibrates. Seeing it's Blake, I slide my finger across the screen and put it to my ear. "What's up?"

"Mom just told me that you're in Oregon with Cybil. What the fuck, Tanner? We have clients coming in a few days. When are you coming back?" he growls, and my temper flares while my hand balls into a fist.

"No 'Is everything okay'? No 'I heard what happened. How's Cybil doing?' Just 'When the fuck are you coming back?'" I walk down the hall when an elderly woman shoots me a look of reprimand for either cursing or speaking loudly. "Who the fuck do you think you're talking to?"

"I'm talking to you, the guy who owns a third of Live Life Adventures, or did you forget about that shit once Cybil showed up?"

"Buy me out."

"W . . . what?" he asks, sounding caught off guard and suddenly calm, but I'm done, so fucking done with his bullshit. I could understand him being upset about Cybil and me meeting during a retreat, but after spending time with us last night, I figured he'd see how happy she makes me and want that for me.

"Get together with Maverick and come up with an offer. If it's acceptable, I'll sign over my portion of the business to you two."

"You'd give everything up for some chick you just met?"

"No, but I'd give it up for the woman I'm falling in love with." I hang up and turn off my cell before I tuck it into my back pocket. When I turn around, Bernard is standing close and wearing a look that shows he just heard my side of that conversation.

Fuck.

"Everything all right?"

"All good," I lie and dip my head toward his coffee. "Did they have whiskey?"

"Nope."

"Sucks," I mutter, hearing him chuckle as we walk back to the waiting room, where we take up two seats near the doors to wait for the girls to get back.

"Normally, I wouldn't do this." He breaks the silence that's settled between us, and I turn my head his way. "Jade's explained to me more than once that things are different nowadays, and that just because a woman is with a man, that doesn't necessarily mean they're in a relationship or that it's serious." He runs a hand down his beard while I try to figure out where he's going with this. "That said, I heard what you said on the phone, so I guess I wanna know if I'm gonna have to prepare my girls for Cybil moving away."

"With all due respect, Cybil and I haven't had a chance to talk about our relationship or our plans. Are things serious on my end? Yes. But I don't know where her head's at, and I don't think right now is the time to discuss our situation."

"Right." He takes a sip of coffee, then rests the paper cup on the top of his thigh. "I gotta warn you: if you hurt her, I'll hurt you."

"I wouldn't expect anything less."

"Be prepared, son." He shakes his head. "Cybil is just like her mama was, sweet to her core and stubborn as hell."

"I can see that," I say, and he looks like he wants to say more but stops, because both Cybil and Jade come around the corner, the two of them with their eyes red and faces blotchy from crying.

When Cybil is close, I push up to stand, and she falls into me, pressing her face into my chest as I wrap my arms around her.

"Mom is asking for you," Jade tells her dad before locking her gaze on Cybil. "You should go home."

"I'm staying," Cybil argues, shaking her head.

"I know being here isn't easy for you."

"It's not, but I'm not leaving," she says stubbornly.

"Cybil—"

"You both should go," Bernard says, cutting the two of them off before they can start quarreling.

"Dad."

"It doesn't make much sense for the two of you to spend the next few hours mostly sitting in the waiting room. You can come back tomorrow when your mom's in her room." He looks at me. "Can you make sure they both get home?"

"Absolutely," I say, and he hugs Jade before Cybil goes to him and wraps her arms around his waist.

"I'll see you all tomorrow."

"Do you want us to bring you dinner or clothes or anything?" Cybil asks.

"No, sweetheart, I'll go home for a little while this evening to shower and pack a bag."

"Are you sure, Dad?" Jade asks, and he lifts an arm out toward her. She steps into him so that she and Cybil are in his embrace.

"I love you, girls, and I'll see you both tomorrow," he says before he lets the two of them go and heads for the hall.

"Do you want to come back to my house for a while?" Cybil asks, looking at Jade, and she shakes her head.

"I think I'm going to open the store, keep my mind off things."

"Then we'll go with you," Cybil says, and Jade looks at me.

"I'm good with whatever you ladies want to do," I say, and she gives me a strange look before transferring it to Cybil.

"He doesn't know your secret," Cybil says, laughing for the first time since Galvin called her today, and Jade grins.

"What am I missing?" I look between the two of them, getting the feeling that they were trouble when they were younger and maybe still are.

"You'll see." Jade nudges my shoulder while Cybil grabs my hand.

"Maybe I should stay with Bernard," I mutter, and the two of them laugh as we head out of the hospital.

Once we're in our rental and out of the parking garage, we head into town, which is small even by small-town standards, with only a couple of fast-food shops and no Target or even Walmart in sight. When we get to Main Street in the middle of town, Cybil directs me to park, then points out the window at a small shop nestled between other buildings. "That's it."

"A bookstore?" I glance at Jade in the rearview mirror, then at Cybil sitting next to me.

"Bound to Please is a little more than a bookstore," Jade informs me as she opens her door and gets out, and I look over at Cybil and raise a brow.

"You'll see." She unhooks her belt, then leans over to the console between us and cups my jaw before kissing me softly. "Thank you for being here with me, for getting me here, and just for being you."

"I wouldn't want to be anywhere else, sunshine," I tell her truthfully, and her face softens.

"Hey, are you two coming?" Jade knocks on the window, and Cybil sighs while letting her hand fall away.

"My best friend is nuts."

"I'm getting the feeling you both are."

"No, she's just a bad influence," she says before looking over my shoulder when Jade knocks again. "We're coming! Sheesh. Calm down." She opens her door as I open mine, and I get out, meeting her at the hood to take her hand. As we reach the entrance to the bookstore, Jade holds open the door for us to enter before her, and once we're inside, I look around, not seeing anything out of the ordinary. Books fill most of the space, with a couch and coffee table under the window in the front and shelves with odds and ends near the register.

"I'll let you take him to the back room," Jade says, heading for the counter, and Cybil leads me to a door with a **Do Not Enter** sign painted on it. She opens it, waiting for me to go in ahead of her.

As I step into the room, it takes a second for it to register that the small room, no bigger than my closet back at home, is filled with sex toys and other X-rated paraphernalia.

"Jade loves books as much as I do," Cybil says, and I turn to face her. "Ever since we were little, she wanted to open a bookstore, but by the time she saved enough money to do it, she realized she wouldn't be able to earn a living from selling paperbacks, so she came up with an idea in order to have her dream."

"It's smart. Does everyone know about this place, or is it a secret all the women in town keep to themselves?"

"Most people know about it," Jade says, leaning against the doorjamb. "Even the mayor, who's about seventy, has come in and bought a few things."

"Don't tell me that!" Cybil cries, shaking her head and following Jade out of the room.

"Hey, everyone needs to have a good time. You should have seen the—"

Jade doesn't have a chance to finish, because Cybil attacks and tries to cover her mouth, causing the two of them to fall to the floor in a pile of laughter. Crossing my arms over my chest, I watch them, shaking my head.

"I missed you." Cybil falls to her back next to Jade while reaching out to grab her hand.

"I missed you, too, but I'm glad you're home." Jade's eyes meet mine and fill with sadness before she sits up and pulls Cybil up with her. "You should take Tanner down the block to Brew's."

"Should I take Tanner to Brew's, or should we go to Brew's and get you a chocolate chip iced latte?"

"I wouldn't be opposed to a chocolate chip latte." She moves behind the counter. "And I would come with you, but I need to call Erin and Jeff and work out a schedule for the rest of the week, since I want to be able to spend as much time as I can with Mom while she's in the hospital."

"All right, do you want anything else from Brew's while we're there?"

"A sandwich, whatever is on special today. Unless it's tuna; then just choose something."

"Got it." Cybil looks at me. "Ready?"

"Yep, lead the way." I place my hand against her lower back, then open the door for her. Once we're outside, she leads me down the block to a small café that's part coffee shop, part deli, and the moment we enter, the entire place grows quiet as everyone turns our way.

"How's Maisie?" the older gentleman behind the register asks, and Cybil's fingers tighten around mine as we step up to the counter.

"She's going to be okay."

"Good." His eyes come to me, then drop to our hands. "Who's your friend?"

"This is Tanner. Tanner, I'd like you to meet Mr. Brew. He owns this place now but used to teach tenth-grade English when I was in school."

"Nice to meet you." I lift my chin.

"You too." His attention goes back to Cybil. "Galvin is in town."

"I know."

"He got married."

"I know that too." Her fingers tighten around mine as he looks between us once more, probably realizing that now is not the time to gossip or dig for information.

"Are you two eating or just getting coffee?"

"Jade wants her usual coffee and the special, as long as it's not tuna. And I'll have a grilled cheese and an iced coffee." She tips her head back toward me. "Mr. Brew's wife makes bread from scratch every day for the sandwiches. Jade always gets the special but swears Thanksgiving on Toast is the best thing here."

"I'll try that then, and a Coke if you've got it," I say, and Mr. Brew jots down our order, saying it will be a few minutes. While our sandwiches are being made, we take our drinks to a small table in the back away from everyone and take a seat.

"Sorry about that."

"About what?" I ask, watching her mix extra sugar into her coffee.

"Him bringing up Galvin." She chews the inside of her cheek. "I think it's weirder for everyone else than it is for me that we aren't together anymore."

"You were together a long time."

"Yeah," she agrees with a sigh, dropping her eyes to her drink.

"Are you going to talk to him?"

"I don't know." She lifts her head and locks her gaze on mine. "I don't think we have anything to talk about, and I don't need him to apologize again. Everything is done. I just want to move forward, you know?"

"I get that." I reach across the table and tuck a piece of hair behind her ear.

"Do you have any advice on how to deal with an ex?"

"No, I've never had an ex to deal with," I say, and she blinks at me, looking stunned.

"You've never had a girlfriend?"

"I never had the time or the inclination to pursue anyone until you showed up. You're the first woman who's made me want more."

"You're being serious." Her eyes scan mine as she shakes her head. "Sorry, it's just hard to believe, because you're *you*."

"Pardon?"

"You're, like . . . the whole package. You're sweet, considerate, super hot, and handy," she says, listing my attributes, and I grin at the word *hot*, which makes her roll her eyes. "Okay, so maybe you're also arrogant, which isn't a great quality to have, but the fact that you could survive in the great outdoors would make up for that if zombies or aliens showed up or something."

"Good to know I'd be useful." I laugh and rub the area over my heart that feels funny hearing her talk about me, and she smiles.

"You're more than just useful, and I'm seriously lucky," she says quietly, and just like that, my decision to sell my part of Live Life Adventures is reinforced, because fuck me if there aren't some things in life that are more important than making money, and one of those things is sitting across from me.

Chapter 20

CYBIL

As I blink my eyes open, it takes a moment for them to adjust to the dark and for my mind to remind me of where I am. Home, only for some reason, it doesn't quite feel like home. I miss Tanner's bed and his house. The only thing that makes being here feel right is that he's here with me.

Unsure what woke me, I reach over to grab my cell, wanting to check the time. My guess is it's early, since it's still dark, but the almost-nonexistent windows in my room and the trees surrounding my house have a tendency to play tricks on you. When I see it's almost three in the morning, I sigh, and Tanner's arm around my waist tightens.

"Are you awake?"

I wait for him to answer, and when he doesn't, I carefully move his arm and maneuver myself off the bed, grabbing a sweater on the way out, since there's a chill in the air, and all I have on is a pair of panties and a thin camisole. After I step out of the room, I carefully shut the door and head down the hall, passing the spare bedroom that I turned into a closet and my tiny office. Since my house isn't actually a house but a small single-wide trailer, it takes mere seconds to reach the kitchen.

After turning on the light over the stove, I grab a glass from the cupboard and get the filtered water from the fridge, filling my glass before guzzling it down and filling it back up. I take my second glass to the door and pull the curtain aside to look across the yard at my shop, the steel building that's three times bigger than my house and the main reason I bought this property, the other being that I'm over a quarter mile from my nearest neighbor.

If I wasn't worried about Tanner waking up and wondering where I went, I would go over there, find some fabric, and start up my sewing machine to help clear my head. Today, or I guess it was yesterday, was mentally exhausting, especially seeing Maisie in the hospital, completely out of it.

"Hey." Tanner's sleepy voice startles me, and I jump slightly, turning to look at him over my shoulder as his arms wrap around my middle.

"You scared me."

"Sorry." His lips touch the space between my neck and shoulder, sending a shiver down my spine. "What woke you up?"

"I don't know," I say quietly, letting the curtain fall back into place. "I think it's a little of everything—Maisie being in the hospital, and just being back here."

"Being back here?" He turns me to face him and smooths my hair back over my shoulder; then his thumb slides back and forth across my jaw. The contact sends tingles across my skin.

"I don't know; it feels strange. But nothing here has changed except me. I don't feel like the same person I was when I left. Does that make sense?"

"I think a lot happened while you were gone, so I can understand why you'd feel different." His hand slips back to my nape, and he squeezes while saying softly, "I also think it's going to take time for people to see that being with Galvin didn't define who you are."

"I think you're right," I agree, knowing my relationship with Galvin has always been the thing people thought of when they saw me, so they don't know what to say or how to act around me now that he and I are no longer together. That's why being with Tanner away from here felt so good. I didn't have to deal with the awkwardness. I was just able to be myself. "We should go back to bed."

With a lift of his chin, he takes the glass from my hand, setting it on the counter before moving me down the hall. When we reach my room, I drop my sweater to the floor and climb into bed. He gets in with me, fitting himself against my back and resting his hand on my stomach, which causes my muscles to bunch and twitch.

"I like your bed," he says quietly, the words brushing my ear and causing my nipples to pebble.

"You and I hardly fit in my bed," I whisper back, covering his hand with mine as I smile. Really, I didn't know if the two of us would be able to fit in my double bed, but somehow, we're making it work.

"That's why I like it. You have nowhere to go, so you can't run from me."

"Hmm," I hum, and his hips push forward, allowing me to feel how hard he is. I press my thighs together to ease the ache between my legs. "I could get away if I wanted to," I say breathlessly, and he lifts the bottom of my camisole, placing his hand against my bare stomach.

"Why would you want to get away from me?" He nips my earlobe, causing a zing of desire and heat to travel down between my legs. With every inch of me waiting in anticipation, I hold my breath, then hiss as his fingers skim just under the edge of my panties, and lower over my pubic bone, then down between the lips of my pussy. Latching onto his arm, I pant for breath as he rolls over my clit.

"You're already soaked, sunshine, and I've hardly touched you." His warm breath causes me to break out in goose bumps while his fingers send me spiraling quickly toward an orgasm.

"Don't stop." I turn my head, and his mouth catches mine. As his tongue slips between my lips, I fall over the edge, moaning his name. I come back to myself as he slows the kiss and rolls me to my back.

"Clothes off." The gruff order leaves no room for argument, not that I would argue with him. I swiftly rid myself of my cami, then lift my hips and slide the cotton material down my thighs before tossing my panties to the end of the bed as he frees himself from his boxers. The moment we're both naked, he grasps my ankles to spread my legs, then crawls up the bed between my legs and looms over me with only the moon making it possible to see him.

"You're beautiful." I slide my hand down his chest and abs, then wrap my hand around his cock, listening to him groan as I stroke him, loving how he feels in my hand.

"Legs around my hips, Cybil." His hand covers mine as I lift my legs; then he guides our hands to my entrance, with me still holding him.

I bite my bottom lip and arch my back off the bed as he enters me, sure there's nothing better in the world than this, than feeling him inside me, feeling him over me, being the center of his attention. Moving my hands to his shoulders, I hold on as he thrusts in and out of me hard, stealing my breath every time he bottoms out. "Oh God," I whimper when tingles begin to dance over my skin and my core starts to tighten.

"I'm right there with you, sunshine." He kisses me slowly, then pulls away and fucks me hard, the sound of skin slapping and heavy breathing filling the room.

"Tanner." I lose myself to the waves of pleasure that he's built, my body becoming liquid, my mind blanking of everything but the tidal wave of pleasure as I come.

"Never had anything better than you in my life, baby. Fuck, I'd give everything up for you and never regret it," he groans, thrusting into me once more before planting himself there. Tears spring to my eyes, and I wrap my arms around his waist and lift up to bury my face against his neck. His words rock me to my core while his heavy weight settles on top of me, making me feel safe rather than suffocated. "I'm heavy, baby," he says quietly.

"Don't move, please," I whisper when he tries to roll away, and I tighten my hold on him. He doesn't say a word. Instead, he gives me what I need. His weight settles back against me, and after a few short minutes, I fall asleep under the man I'm falling in love with, feeling safer and more complete than I have in years.

I wake with a start, the sound of what my sleepy brain registered as a gunshot still ringing in my ears. With my heart pounding, I roll over to search for Tanner, but the bed is empty, as is the bathroom, which I can see from where I am.

"Tanner?"

Silence greets my ears, and my heart drops to my stomach as I quickly get off the bed to search the floor for my clothes, trying to listen for anything out of the ordinary as I put them on. With my hands now shaking, I open the door and step out into the hallway. I can't see or hear anything, but I do smell something burning, so I rush to the kitchen and turn off the stove, where a single pancake is burnt to a crisp.

Hearing voices coming from outside, I go to the front door and pull the curtain aside, blinking in disbelief at what I see. Earl, my seventy-plus-year-old neighbor who looks like the lumberjack version of Santa, has his handgun aimed at a shirtless Tanner, who's got a bag of garbage in his hand. Without thinking, I swing the front door open, then scream as Earl lifts the barrel in my direction and fires a shot into the air over the top of my trailer. Startled, I slip off the step I'm standing on and land on my ass at the bottom of the stairs, watching in horror as Tanner rushes Earl.

"No, Tanner, don't hurt him!" I yell over the sound of the blood now thundering through my veins. Thankfully, he slows down, but he's still quick enough to disarm my neighbor in one smooth move, tucking the gun in the back of his unbuttoned jeans before stalking back toward me.

"Sunshine, what the fuck were you thinking?" he asks, hunching down next to me and moving his hand over my head and limbs. Just as I start to tell him I'm okay, he stands, pulling me up with him and wrapping his arms around me so tightly that all the air in my lungs leaves in a whoosh.

"Are you all right, Cybil? I thought this guy was robbing you," Earl says, sounding nervous.

"I told you I fucking wasn't robbing her," Tanner rumbles, and I try to wiggle to get free, sure that I'm going to pass out from being held so tightly.

"How was I to know you weren't lying? Cybil's Bronco isn't here, and I've never seen you before."

"I explained to you why that was, old man!" Tanner yells, making me jump, and his hold tightens even more.

"I . . . I can't breathe," I choke out as stars begin to float through my vision.

"Shit, sorry." He lets me go, and I gulp in air while watching Earl fiddle with the brim of his hat in his hands.

"I'm okay," I assure both men once I've caught my breath, but neither of them looks appeased. "Really, I'm fine."

"You're shaking and pale," Tanner informs me before glaring at Earl. "What the fuck were you thinking, shooting in her direction?"

"I didn't know it was her. I thought she was someone helping you rob the place."

"Right, because it's normal for people to commit acts of burglary while shirtless and to also stop and take out the trash on their way out."

"I don't like your tone, son," Earl rumbles, his face getting red with either embarrassment or anger. Probably a little of both, knowing him.

"Yeah, well, I don't like my girlfriend getting shot at." Tanner turns to face me and lifts his finger. "Don't ever do that again!" he growls, and my jaw goes slack.

"W-what?" I hold my hand to my chest. "I didn't get shot at on purpose."

"You shouldn't have come outside like you did," Earl says, reprimanding me, and I toss my arms in the air.

"You're both obviously deluded, because none of this is my fault."

"If you had called to let me know you were home, I wouldn't have worried when I drove by and saw that car outside or when I saw him leaving your house with a garbage bag," Earl says, and Tanner makes a sound in the back of his throat that I take to mean he's agreeing with him.

"Unbelievable." I shake my head, looking between the two of them. "I'm not doing this." I turn on my heel and head into the house, leaving them standing outside. Annoyed and in need of caffeine, I go to the kitchen and grab a coffee mug from the cupboard, then slam it down on the counter with a little too much force, causing the handle to break off in my hand. Cursing under my breath, I toss the broken pieces into the trash, then grab a new one, fill it with coffee, and get my creamer from the fridge.

"Sunshine," Tanner calls, but I don't bother responding to the endearment that normally makes my heart flutter. Instead, I focus on dumping creamer into my cup. "You're pissed."

"No, I'm annoyed that you and Earl decided to gang up on me," I inform him, and he laughs. "I'm glad I can entertain you." I take a sip of my coffee.

"I didn't mean to laugh. It's not funny that you're annoyed." He comes to me, taking the mug from my hand and placing it on the counter before cupping my face in his palms. "You're just very cute." His lips brush across mine, and when my lashes flutter open, he slides his fingers back into my hair. "I shouldn't have yelled at you. I just lost my mind when I saw that gun pointed in your direction."

"I kind of got that." I rest my hands against his chest, biting back the urge to bring up the fact that none of this was my fault. "Is Earl still outside?"

"Do you mean your very overprotective neighbor?" He skims his nose down mine. "Because that guy is still outside in the driveway, waiting for you to come out and give him a hug. His words, not mine."

"I should go out there." I sigh, shaking my head.

"While you do that, I'm going to make us breakfast." He places a swift kiss against my lips, then lets me go.

Going to the door, I open it slowly, then step outside with my hands up. "Don't shoot."

"Such a smart-ass," Earl mutters, while I hear Tanner inside start to laugh, obviously no longer angry about the whole "getting shot at" business.

"Just being cautious." I head down the steps, and Earl opens his arms wide.

"You know most people get a fridge magnet or key chain when they go on a trip, not a man," he says as I wrap my arms around his burly waist and rest the side of my head against his chest.

"Well, those people aren't going on the right kind of trips." I tip my head back and grin up at him, watching as he shakes his head.

"It's good to have you back, kid."

"Yeah." I step back when he lets me go. "Do you have dinner plans tonight?"

"Not that I know of."

"Well, now you do, with Tanner and me." I motion to the trailer. "We can grill out tonight."

"Does your new guy eat meat?"

"He does, but I'm still going to make vegetables." I plant my hands on my hips. "You know you're worse than a kid when it comes to eating things that are good for you."

"The point is I'm no longer a kid, which means I get to eat what I like, when I like." He smiles, causing his beard to shift on his face and the wrinkles around his eyes to stand out even more.

"Fine." I roll my eyes. "How about between six thirty and seven?"

"I'll be here." He pulls his keys out of his pocket. "Let Tanner know I'll bring a case of beer, since I know you don't got any."

"So you two are on a first-name basis now?"

"He's a military man and protective of you. He has my respect," he says, and my heart warms, because that means a lot coming from Earl, since he didn't even like Galvin, and he knew him for years. "See you tonight." He gets in his truck, and I stand back, waving as he drives off, then head inside, finding Tanner at the stove.

"Earl's going to come over for dinner tonight."

"Good, I'd like to pick his brain about some stuff," he says, flipping over a pancake, and I frown.

"What kind of stuff?" I hop up on the counter next to the stove and pick up my coffee to take a sip.

"Work in the area, that kind of thing."

"What?" I frown at the side of his head. "Why would you want to know about work when you have a job back home in Montana?"

"I'm selling my portion of Live Life to the guys," he replies, and my stomach bottoms out while my chest starts to feel funny.

"I don't understand." I shake my head. "When did that happen?"

"Yesterday."

Yesterday? Yesterday, after he left Montana to fly with me to Oregon?

"You told me that you love your job and that Maverick and Blake are your family."

"Shit changes." I watch his jaw flex as he shrugs. Seeing that and knowing how Blake felt about Tanner and me getting together, and Tanner now here with me, I can't help but wonder if this is all my fault.

"Tanner, I—"

"Don't, Cybil," he says, cutting me off before I can tell him that he needs to really think about this. "We need to eat breakfast; then you should call Bernard to see if Maisie's been moved to her room so you can go spend some time with her."

Chewing the inside of my cheek, I study him for a long moment, trying to figure out what to say, but the waves of frustration or anger coming off him are not making me feel like he'd be open to me saying anything at all. "Okay," I say, giving in, and he nods once before looking at me and cupping my jaw.

"It will be okay."

"Sure," I agree, not believing him but praying he's right.

Chapter 21

Cybil

Hand in hand with Tanner, I knock on the door to Maisie's room and peek my head in, seeing a nurse standing next to her bed, with Bernard asleep, taking up the chair next to it. "Is it all right for us to come in?" I whisper when her eyes meet mine.

"Yep, I just finished up." She shoots me a smile before taking in the man at my side, getting a look of appreciation on her face that I've seen from other women when they come face to face with Tanner. Hell, I'm pretty sure I had that look the first time I saw him in all his glory.

"How's she doing today?" I ask quietly, stepping farther into the room.

"She's doing great," she assures me as I let go of Tanner's hand and take the flowers he's carrying in one arm. I set them on the stand under the TV before making my way to the bed. The nurse leaves, wheeling her cart out of the room.

"Hey," I say quietly when Bernard opens his eyes, and he smiles at me before he looks over at Maisie and sits up.

"I must have fallen asleep."

"I'm sure you're tired." I lean over to place a kiss on his cheek. "Tanner and I are going to be here for a while, if you want to go stretch your legs and get a coffee."

"Thanks, sweetheart." He stands, rubbing my shoulder before patting Tanner on the back. "I'll be back in a few minutes."

"Take your time." I watch him leave, then take a seat in his chair and pick up Maisie's hand while Tanner sits on the AC vent next to me. Since his admission this morning, I've found out absolutely nothing about why he's decided to sell his part of Live Life Adventures. But I have found out he's not open to talking about it. And I know this because when I tried to bring it up while we were showering, he avoided the conversation by distracting me with a kiss before fucking me against the wall. It worked, but then again, when it comes to him, I'm apparently weak.

"Hey, sweet girl." Maisie's fingers tightening around mine bring me out of my head, and I focus on her sleepy pale face.

"Hey." I get up and lean over the rail on the bed to kiss her cheek; then I lean back and glance quickly over my shoulder. "I want you to meet someone."

"Tanner." She smiles tiredly as he walks around to the opposite side of the bed and bends to kiss her cheek.

"It's nice to meet you, ma'am."

"Please call me Maisie. *Ma'am* makes me feel old, when I already feel ancient lying in this hospital bed." She pats his hand, resting on the side of the bed, then turns her head toward me. "I've missed you, pretty girl."

"I missed you too." Tears cloud my vision, and she forces me to release her hand, then cups my cheek.

"No tears."

"I can't help it." I cover her hand with mine and close my eyes. Pain lances through my chest as I flash back to being in this exact position with my mom on more than one occasion. I don't know what I would do if I lost Maisie.

"Look at me, sweetheart," she orders, and I blink my eyes open to meet her gaze. "I'm okay, and I'm going to be just fine."

"I know," I say quietly, and she nods, then looks between Tanner and me. "Now, with you both here, I want to hear everything that happened on your adventure and how you two ended up together."

I listen to Tanner laugh, and I smile.

"There's a lot to tell you."

"Well, I have a lot of time," she says, so I dive into the story of how we met and everything that went on after.

Halfway through the story of when I found out Tanner would be my partner for the week, Bernard comes back, with Jade in tow. They pull up chairs and listen to me tell Maisie about everything that happened, including all the beautiful places we visited, Oliver and Lauren's arguments and escapades, getting lost and then shot at by poachers, and everything in between. By the time I finish, the three of them are staring at me like they've never seen me before. Then again, they haven't; I used to always stick close to home, and I never really took any unnecessary risks.

"Well, that Lauren woman sounds horrible, but I have to say she redeemed herself by helping you when you sliced your hand open," Maisie says, shaking her head and smiling.

"I'm not even a little surprised you put up a tent on your own just to prove a point to her," Jade says with a laugh.

"Are we going to talk about her getting shot at?" Bernard asks, and I smile at him.

"No, Tanner doesn't like to talk about me getting shot at."

"You say that like it's happened more than once." He frowns and I smile.

"Well, this morning, Tanner was taking out the trash when Earl came over to check on my place. He thought Tanner was robbing me, and he pulled a gun on him."

"Oh shit," Jade breathes, and I look at her and nod.

"I know, and when I opened the door and stepped outside, he shot over the top of my trailer, scaring me so badly I fell down the steps."

"Oh my," Maisie whispers, and I pat her hand.

"I'm all right."

"Child, you have the worst luck," Bernard says, then looks at Tanner. "You're going to have your work cut out, keeping her safe."

"I'm starting to figure that out," Tanner replies with a smile in his voice, and I turn to grin at him. His face softens as he reaches out to touch my cheek with the tips of his fingers.

"I think I need to sign up for a Montana adventure," Jade says wistfully.

"It really was the best time, even with everything that happened." I laugh, then look at Maisie when she yawns. "Are you tired?"

"Unfortunately." She reaches for Bernard's hand, turning his way. "Why don't you go home and get some sleep? I know you didn't get much last night with the doctors and nurses in and out of my room constantly."

"I'm all right. Plus, I wouldn't be able to sleep without you anyway." He kisses the top of her hand, then glances between Jade and me. "What are you two up to today?"

"I don't have plans. I was just going to hang here with Mom."

"You have a business to run, and all I'm going to be doing is sleeping."

"I got Jeff to cover the store, so I have the day off. I don't mind hanging around."

"I do mind," Maisie says in that motherly tone of hers. "I'm sure when I get home in a few days I'll be able to use you girls' help. But right now, I'm being taken care of, so go to work or do something—I don't want you guys hanging around all day." I want to be upset that she wants us gone, but I remember that my mom used to do the same thing when she had to stay in the hospital. She hated me seeing her lying in a bed and hooked up to machines.

"You can come help me pack up orders; then we can bring lunch back here after we drop them off at the post office," I suggest, locking eyes with Jade.

"Okay, sure, if Tanner doesn't mind me tagging along with you two."

"Not at all," he says, getting up.

That settled, I push up from my chair so I can lean over and give Maisie a hug.

"Get some rest, and we'll be back."

"Okay, sweetheart." She lets me go with a kiss to my cheek, and I turn to give Bernard a hug. I take Tanner's hand and leave the room, with Jade following behind after hugging both her parents.

"Do you want to ride with us and leave your car so you don't have to pay for parking twice?" I ask Jade when we get into the elevator inside the parking garage.

"No, I'll meet you two at the house. I'm going to stop by the bookstore to check on Jeff. Do you want me to bring you a coffee from Brew's?"

"You know the way to my heart." I smile, and she laughs as the doors open on the floor where she parked.

"What would you like, Tanner? Wait, don't tell me." She holds up a hand while keeping the doors open with the other one. "Hot coffee, black, no sugar."

"Iced coffee, cream and sugar." Tanner grins.

"Well, aren't you just full of surprises." She gives me a look, then backs out. "See you two in an hour, tops."

"See you in an hour." I wave goodbye to her as the doors close, then lean into Tanner's side and let out a deep breath.

"You doing okay, sunshine?" he asks softly, sliding his arm around my waist while resting his lips on the top of my head.

"Yeah, the last few days have just felt like a whirlwind," I admit as the doors open. I start to step off, but I stop when Galvin and Chris come around the corner. Like yesterday, seeing them together doesn't make me feel hurt or angry; it just makes me feel stupid. It's obvious to me now that they love each other and probably always have. If I hadn't been so blind to the truth, I would have recognized that Chris's dislike for me was actually jealousy and that Galvin's insistence on keeping us separated was because he was trying to protect the man he loves.

"Hey, guys." Galvin breaks the silence, looking between Tanner and me, and I catch Chris step closer to his side, as if to protect him from me. "Are you two going to see Maisie?"

"We're just heading out," I say, leaving out that Maisie was getting tired. Even exhausted, I know she'll be happy to see him. Like me, she kind of adopted him while we were all growing up, so she might have been upset about what happened between us, but that doesn't mean she doesn't still love him. And given what I know of his parents' reaction to him marrying Chris, I'm glad he still has Maisie and Bernard.

Bernard is still angry on my behalf, but I'm sure he'll get over it.

"Have a good visit." I duck around Chris, pulling Tanner with me out of the elevator.

When the doors close behind us, I wonder if we'll ever get back to a place where we can be friends, where he doesn't feel like a complete stranger. Something tells me the answer to that question is no, not with the history between us, and that is possibly more upsetting than anything else, because I do miss him. Or I miss his friendship, even after what he did.

Sitting outside on the floating deck next to my trailer, the stars twinkling above us and the moon out in all its glory, I pick up my iced tea to take a sip. Today was another busy day. It took Jade, Tanner, and me four hours to get things sorted in my shop and the orders that had backed up while I was away packaged up to be sent out. When we were finished, I mailed everything off; then we picked up lunch and went back to the hospital. Maisie was pretty tired, so after we ate lunch with Bernard, we left and went to the grocery store to get the stuff for dinner.

By the time we got home, Earl was pulling in, so while Jade and I made a salad and sautéed potatoes, Tanner and Earl started up the grill.

Now, with my feet tucked under me in my chair and my belly full, I watch Tanner smile as he talks about the lodge, Maverick, Blake, and his family. I know logically I shouldn't feel guilty about his decision to sell because it's his choice, but I still do. It's obvious to anyone listening to him that he loves his job and his family in Montana, even with whatever's gone down.

"When do you have to go back?" Jade asks him, and I hold my breath as I wait for him to answer, because he hasn't talked to me about leaving or staying. He hasn't talked to me about anything.

"Not sure yet." He looks at Earl, and I wonder if he opened up to him or asked him about finding work here.

"You don't have to get back to work?" Jade says with a frown, and I swear I want to kick my best friend when Tanner's jaw twitches.

"I'm here as long as Cybil needs me. We'll figure things out after that."

"How are you two going to make this work? I mean, you live there, and Cybil lives here."

"Jade," I snap, and her eyes come to me. "Stop."

"I was just wondering."

"I know, and as soon as Tanner and I figure things out, you'll know our plans."

"Fine." She pushes back from the table and stands. "I should probably go. With Mom not wanting me hanging around the hospital, I'm going to open the store tomorrow."

"Sure." I get up and give her a hug, ignoring the fact that she's mad at me for not letting her interrogate Tanner. As much as I love her, it's not her place. "Call me tomorrow and let me know when you're going to the hospital, and I'll go with you or meet you there."

"All right." She stoops to kiss Earl's cheek, then waves at Tanner before heading for her car.

"She's just protective of you," Earl says, and I pull my eyes off Jade's car as she drives down my lane and focus on him. "And my guess is she's scared you're going to move away."

"I know." I sigh, watching him get up.

"Do you want me to help you clean up?"

"No, there isn't much to do," I assure him, and he comes over to give me a hug, then pats Tanner's shoulder before wandering to his truck and getting in. When he drives off, I look at Tanner and wait for him to say something—anything—but he doesn't.

Annoyed, or maybe hurt by his lack of communication, I pick up the glasses on the table and take them inside, then start to go back out to get the rest of the dishes, but Tanner walks in with them. "Thanks." I take them from him and put everything into the dishwasher while he stands with his arms crossed over his chest, leaning against the counter.

"Cybil."

"Yeah?" I wait for him to say something, but instead, he shakes his head.

"Nothing, never mind."

"Right." I grab a couple of Tylenols for the headache I feel coming on and swallow them down, with Tanner watching me. "I think I'm going to head to bed early and maybe watch some TV."

"I'll meet you in there in a bit. I'm gonna make a couple of phone calls," he says, and I nod, then go down the hall to my room, where I change into a pair of sleep shorts and a tank top, brush my teeth, and get into bed.

With the TV on, I lie in the dark, trying to figure out what to do. I feel like this whole thing with him and his job is hanging over our relationship, and with him not wanting to talk to me about it, I can only assume I'm somehow responsible for what went down.

"Screw this." I toss back the covers and get out of bed, deciding that one way or another, I'm going to get him to open up. After grabbing my sweater, I open the door and start to head down the hall but stop when I hear him talking to someone.

"You think I like this any more than you, man? Fuck! You of all people know that starting Live Life was a dream for me, but I won't choose between Cybil and that." He pauses as I get closer, and I know I should make my presence known, but my mouth has gone dry. "I don't give a fuck. That's on him; that's not on me. He needs to get his shit together." Another long pause. "Right, well, let me know what the lawyer says, and we'll talk after that. Later, brother." He hangs up and turns toward me, putting his cell phone into his pocket.

As his haunted gaze meets mine, my stomach rolls and my legs start to feel weak. "You're selling because of me." I knew that, or I thought I did, but having it confirmed feels like a knife to the gut.

"Not just you."

"Really?" I tip my head to the side while wrapping my arms around my waist. "So if we didn't meet, you were planning on offering up your portion to Blake and Maverick?"

"No."

His simple answers to my questions make me want to shake him.

"So, what is it? Are you selling because of me, or because you decided that it's no longer your dream and you now want to be on the first trip to Mars?"

"Don't be a smart-ass, Cybil."

"Don't be a liar, Tanner." I shake my head, realizing everything that's against us and all he would be giving up because of me. I know he might think he's made the right decision now, but in a week, a month, or a few years, he's going to end up resenting me. I just can't stand the thought of that. I mean, look what happened with Galvin, who was living a lie and dragging me along for a ride I didn't know I was on. And in the end I was the one who got hurt. "I can't do this."

"What?" He takes a step toward me, and I hold up my hand to ward him off.

"I mean, I can't do this. I don't know what I was thinking, or maybe I wasn't thinking." I want to shove the words back in my mouth as soon as they're out, but I need to end this before it's too late, before he throws away everything he's worked for, and before I fall any deeper in love with him. Shit, I love him—the realization makes my chest hurt and the lie I spit out taste bitter. "We don't work. This"—I motion between us—"is never going to work."

"Don't do this, Cybil," he bites out, and I swallow.

"You know I'm right."

"What I know is that you think you're protecting me, when you're not. You're just pissing me off."

"No, I'm being realistic," I say quietly, ignoring the fact that my throat is starting to burn. "You need to go back to Montana, and I need to get back to my life here."

"All right." He crosses his arms over his chest and leans back like he's settling in. "If you're set on doing this, I want you to give me one good reason why I should walk away."

I stare at him, my mind scrambling for something, anything, but it's difficult, especially when I thought he would just leave.

"I'm waiting."

"You eat meat," I blurt out, the first thing that comes to mind, and he laughs.

No, he doesn't just laugh. His head falls back on his shoulders and he roars his amusement.

"This is not funny."

"Yes, it is." He shakes his head, still chuckling. "Okay, so what else?"

What else? There's nothing else, and that was hard enough to come up with. "You said one thing."

"Your one thing was lame, so unless you can come up with something else, I'm not going anywhere."

"Why are you making this so difficult?" I stomp my foot like I'm a three-year-old not getting her way, and he grins.

"Because what we have is worth it, and I know you'll end up regretting ending things about five minutes after I walk out the door, because you're in love with me."

I gasp and take a step back. "I don't love you."

"You're really on a roll tonight. First, you try to break up with me, then you lie to my face." He makes a *tsk-tsk* sound while shaking his finger back and forth. "You love me, Cybil, and just because you're not willing to admit it out loud doesn't make it any less true." His arms fall to his sides, and he steps toward me. "We're not breaking up, and I'm not going anywhere unless you're going with me."

"Tanner." Tears cloud my vision as he wraps his hand around the side of my neck, the other around my hip. "You . . ." I swallow hard. "You giving up your dream because of me is too heavy a weight for me to carry around on my shoulders, especially when we hardly know each other."

"Sunshine, if I don't have you, none of the other shit will even matter, and yeah, we are still getting to know each other, but time isn't going to change how I feel about you," he says gently, urging me closer until my body is pressed against his. "I love that you want to protect me, but I know what I want and what I need." Both his hands grasp my face as he cups my jaw. "We have enough to deal with, and a lot of shit to figure out, so let's not make things more complicated than they already are by fighting."

"I need you to talk to me about stuff. If this is going to work, we need to be honest with each other, even when it's stuff we don't want to talk about."

"I can do that."

"Okay," I say quietly, and he leans down, pressing his lips to mine in a soft, sweet kiss. When he pulls back, he studies me for a long moment, then rests his forehead against mine.

"I love you, sunshine."

My breath catches while my hands latch onto the front of his shirt.

"I know a lot has happened. I know this is all new, but everything's going to be all right as long as we trust each other," he tells me gently.

"I just don't want you to end up hating me," I admit, dropping my eyes from his.

"Look at me, Cybil," he urges, using his thumbs to lift my chin. "I'm not going to hate you, and shit with Blake has been brewing for a while, and that shit has nothing to do with you."

"What does that mean?" I wait, expecting him to blow off my question or to distract me like he's done before, so I'm shocked when he doesn't.

"He thinks working himself to death will earn his dad's respect." His jaw clenches. "He doesn't realize the reason his dad is pissed at him all the time isn't because he's not good enough but because he's disappointed Blake's forgotten what's actually important in life." He lets out a deep breath.

"Over the last couple of years, things with him have gotten progressively worse. He's forgotten what we fought for while we were in the military and why we built Live Life to begin with. We didn't do it for the money. We did it because we wanted to make a difference. We wanted to help people realize their potential, to show them how strong they are, and to build bonds like the one we share." His voice drops. "We wanted to do something that made us feel like we were still giving back. He might have forgotten that, but I haven't, and neither has Maverick."

Hearing that, I want to shake Blake myself. "Have you talked to him? I mean, I know it's not exactly normal protocol for men to use more than a few words at a time." He smirks as I add, "But have you ever told him how you feel?"

"Not in so many words." He laughs when I roll my eyes. "Besides, it doesn't matter anymore. You're here. Your family and friends are here, and I know you won't want to move."

"You know that, do you?" I raise a brow.

"You wanna move to Montana?" he asks, and my heart starts to speed up. The idea of leaving Jade, Maisie, and Bernard makes me feel slightly nauseous, but the truth is I would move to be with him.

"No," I say, and he tries to hide his disappointment. "Not right now with everything that happened to Maisie, but once I know she's going to be okay, yes. Absolutely."

"Really?"

"I love your house."

"And?"

"And what?" I frown.

"And I love you."

"Thanks." I press my lips together to keep from laughing, then scream and take off in a run, shrieking as he chases me down the hall and into my room.

"Trapped with nowhere to go." He closes the door and stands in front of it. "I'm not letting you leave this room until I hear you say 'I love you, Tanner.'" He stalks toward me, then catches me around the waist when I attempt to get across the bed.

"Tanner," I breathe as his weight settles between my legs.

"Yeah, sunshine?" His lips brush mine.

"Never mind," I gasp as he kisses me.

And sometime later, after he's pushed me to the edge and fallen over with me, I wrap my arms around him and whisper "I love you" against his ear, thankful he didn't let me give up on us.

Chapter 22

Tanner

With Cybil still asleep after I've taken a shower, I quietly leave the bedroom, head down the hall to the kitchen, and flip on the coffeepot before going to the living room to turn on the news. I start to take a seat on the couch, but my cell phone buzzes on the counter. I grab it and see a text from Blake, asking me to call him.

After Cybil tried to break up with me last night because of this situation with him, I'm not feeling very amicable, but at the end of the day, he's still my brother. Not sure how this call will go, I take my phone with me outside in case I lose my shit like I have the last couple of times we've spoken. I clear the last step, head across the grass to the floating deck that's kitty-corner to the edge of the trailer, and take a seat at the table situated near the gas grill. After dialing Blake back, I listen to the phone ring.

"Hey," he answers, sounding out of breath, and I remember that supplies were scheduled to be delivered this morning, so he's probably at the lodge, unloading the truck.

"I got your text. What's up?"

"I'm sorry." I'm caught off guard, and my fingers curl around my cell. "I fucked up. I shouldn't have . . . fuck, I shouldn't have said anything to you, especially in regard to Cybil. And I really shouldn't have been a dick when you took off to be with her after her mom had a heart attack," he says, and I don't correct him about Maisie being her mom, since she is Cybil's mother figure, even if she doesn't call her Mom. "I just . . . shit. Everything between you and her happened so fast; then you took off, and I didn't take it well."

"You know I love you like a brother, man, but I'm done with the bullshit. I'm not going to live my life waiting for the next time you slip up and say some shit that will piss me off. Especially when your anger has nothing to do with me, or Mav, or the business. I also do not need to explain my relationship to you or justify why I'm leaving or need time off. I don't work for you. I work *with* you, and as my friend, you should want me to be happy."

"You're right. You're a hundred percent right." He gives in immediately, and I wonder what the fuck is going on.

"Why are you having a change of attitude about this now?"

"Let's just say I've had everyone up in my face for the last few days, pointing out how I fucked up and letting me know I need to fix shit or they're done with me."

"You deserve that."

"I know," he agrees quietly, then sighs. "I don't want to buy you out, and I don't want to lose you, man—come back."

"I don't know. You're going to have to give me a couple of days to think about things."

"All right. Before you hang up, how's Cybil doing? Is she hanging in there?"

"She's good. She'll be happy we spoke about shit."

"Yeah, so will Mom. She's been on my case since the day you and Cybil took off and I lost my shit."

"She's been on your case for a lot longer than that."

"You're not wrong," he mutters. "Call when you decide, but whatever happens, just know we're still family—that's never going to change."

"Yeah." My stomach muscles tighten. "We'll talk soon." I hang up and drop my head back to my shoulders.

After that phone call and Cybil saying last night that she loved my house and would be willing to move to Montana, everything is back up in the air. I thought I had shit figured out, had already mentally started making plans for making this place a little more comfortable, and had put out some feelers to see about opening my own guide business in the area.

"You look deep in thought." Cybil's words bring me out of my head, and I turn her way and watch her walk across the grass, looking too beautiful in the early-morning light. Her hair's a mess, and the long sweater she has wrapped around her barely hides the fact that she's only wearing a tank top and panties.

"I just got off the phone with Blake," I tell her, reaching for her hand and pulling her down to sit sideways on my lap. "He called to apologize for being a dick."

"That's good." Her eyes study mine as her fingers skim along my jaw, then over my bottom lip.

"It is." I grab hold of her wrist and kiss her fingers before holding her hand against my chest, over my heart. "But after talking to him, you and I need to decide what we're going to do."

"What do you mean?"

"We need to figure out if I'm going to sell and move here, or if you're going to move to Montana with me so we can start our life there."

"Oh," she says quietly, her eyes going from her trailer to her shop, then the trees surrounding us.

Cupping her cheek, I wait for her gaze to come back to me. "If we decide on Montana, you don't have to sell this place—you can keep it, and we can use it when we come to visit, or you can rent it out for a little extra cash or even sell it later on down the road."

"I love you." She rests her forehead on my chin.

Fuck, I don't know if I'll ever get used to or tired of her saying she loves me. Yeah, I've had Mav and Blake, along with his family, but until her, I've never had anyone of my own, and it feels good, better than good, to have someone to belong to. "I love you too."

"I know that it'll take Jade, Maisie, and Bernard time to get used to me being away, but I . . ." She lets out a breath. "But I was happy with you in Montana. It felt like home when I was there, and even though I'm going to miss everyone, I'm ready for a change."

"You sure about that?"

"Would you sell your house and move here if I told you that I didn't want to leave?"

"Yes." I don't even have to think about it. I never wanted to sell my portion of the business, but I would choose Cybil every single time.

"I know you would, so I need you to have as much faith in me as I have in you." She lets out a deep breath, then presses her forehead into the crook of my neck and wraps her arms around me, holding on tight. "I trust you."

"That means a lot, sunshine." I hold her tight, knowing that no matter what happens, as long as she and I find our way through this together, everything else will be all right.

Hearing the engine of Dave's plane start up, I look down at Cybil and wonder if I'm making the right decision. Being away from her isn't something I want, and I know she doesn't want it either. But after lots of conversations and talking to Maisie, Bernard, and Jade, we decided that I would go back to Montana to work. She would join me in a month—enough time to get the rest of her place packed up and on the market.

That doesn't mean it will be easy being away from her, especially after spending the last few weeks together, day in and day out. As I look into her eyes, I realize the next month is going to test our relationship, specifically with me being away from my cell and not contacting her while I'm out with clients.

"I love you." Her chin trembles as she tips her head back to look up at me.

"I love you, too, sunshine." I brush my lips across hers, trying to force myself to release her when everything in me is screaming to hold on tighter and never let her go. "One month."

"One month," she repeats, taking a step back with her fingers still curled around my tee at my sides.

"Be good," I order, and her lips curl up into a smile.

"I will be."

I have no doubt, but it doesn't make this any easier, and it also makes me realize how every taken man I was stationed with felt when they had to leave the lives they had behind in order to go out and fight for the country they loved.

"I'll see you in a month," she says.

"You will." I kiss her once more, this time thrusting my tongue between her lips and dipping her back over my arm. When I come up for air, I look into her eyes, knowing without a doubt that this is going to work, that even if everything else turns to shit, we will be solid. We've found something within each other that neither of us was looking for, but it's impossible to deny, and outside of that, nothing else matters. "See you in thirty days?"

"You will." She lets me go, then gives me a smile. "Remember, I love your house."

"I don't care why you come back to me," I tell her, and her face softens.

"Call me when you land." She takes another step back, and I let her. With her out of reach, I turn and head for the open door of the small plane that will take me home, then stop to look at her once more. Seeing her looking so small and unsure, it kills me to hop into the empty passenger seat and wave goodbye to her. I know she's nervous about what's to come, and so am I. But I also know this is the beginning of our future.

Chapter 23

CYBIL

Standing in the doorway of my shop, I look around the empty space, feeling scared to death and full of hope for what's to come. Tomorrow, Bernard, Maisie, Jade, and I are driving my clothes and other personal items to Montana, with all the stuff from my shop arriving a few days after we get there. Tanner wanted me to wait a few days so he could fly down and drive up with me, but I'm over being away from him, and after a month, even one more day feels like too much time.

When I hear a car pull up behind me, I flip off the lights in the shop and close the door before turning to see who's here. I expect to see Earl, since he said he was going to stop by to say goodbye, but I'm surprised to find Galvin getting out of his car.

"Hey." He tucks his hands in the pockets of his jeans as he walks toward me. "Do you have a minute to talk?"

Part of me wants to say no, but I know I need to get this over with, because tomorrow when I leave, I want to know that my past is in the past, where it should be. "Sure." I walk to the deck and take a seat on the edge of it, and he comes to sit down next to me.

"So you're really leaving tomorrow?"

"I am." My fingers fidget with a thread on the bottom of my jean shorts. "What about you? Are you sticking around town?"

"I have to finish up a few things here; then Chris and I will be heading to Seattle next month."

"You always did love Seattle," I say quietly, and he startles me by grabbing my hand.

"I'm sorry, Cybil, so fucking sorry. I know I said it before, but I want you to know I didn't want to hurt you. I never meant to hurt you."

"I know," I reply as my nose starts to sting.

"My one regret in everything that happened is that I didn't trust you enough to tell you the truth, especially when you're the one person I should have trusted." His fingers squeeze mine. "It was selfish of me to drag you into that. I just . . . I wasn't in a good place, and I was just scared, because I knew choosing Chris would mean losing everyone else I loved."

"I wish you would have trusted me," I whisper as tears I can't control fill my eyes. "You could have trusted me."

"I know." His voice cracks, and I turn to look at him. When his eyes meet mine, I hate the pain I see in his gaze. "Do you think you might be able to forgive me someday?"

"I already forgave you." I let out a deep breath, then rest my head on his shoulder. "Have you talked to your parents?"

"No," he says quietly, and I squeeze my eyes closed. "I'm learning to accept that they might never come around."

"I hate that for you."

"It's a sacrifice I'm willing to make." I feel his lips at the top of my head; then his hand lets go of mine so he can wrap his arm around my shoulders. "Are you happy?"

"Happier than I have ever been. Not that I didn't love you, but—"

"I get it. You don't have to explain being soul-deep in love with someone to me."

"I guess I don't." I lift my head from his shoulder and turn toward him. "Life is funny. Who would have thought that, after years together, we'd be sitting outside my house talking about starting lives with other people?"

"Yeah," he says with a laugh, and I can't help but smile.

I stand up and shake my head as he looks up at me. It's strange to think that his decision to end things between us, a decision that devastated me at the time, was the best thing he could have done—not just for him, but also for me. If he hadn't, I might not have had the chance to fall in love, really fall in love, with a man who loves me so completely. "Thank you."

"For what?" He stands, and I tip my head back to look up at him.

"For being brave enough to follow your heart. I know that wasn't easy for you." I lean toward him, and like a million times before, he opens his arms to me, and I rest my ear against his chest. "I want nothing but happiness for you."

"I know." His chin rests against the top of my head. "And you should tell that guy of yours that if he hurts you, I'll be first in line to kick his ass."

"I'll let him know, as long as you tell Chris the same thing," I say, and his arms around me tighten before he lets me go and takes a step back.

"Promise you'll message me from time to time to let me know how you're doing?"

"I will." I clear my throat in an attempt to fight back the tears I feel creeping up my throat once again.

"I still love you. I know I shouldn't say that to you, but I still do." His eyes drop to his feet for a moment before he lifts his head to look at me once more. "I hope you get everything you ever wanted."

Not trusting myself to not start sobbing, I nod, and he nods back before pulling his keys out of his pocket and heading to his car.

When he gets in behind the wheel, I lift my hand to wave, and he waves back before doing a three-point turn and taking off down the lane. As his taillights disappear out of sight, I look around, then head into my trailer to finish packing, feeling lighter than I have in weeks. Even a tad bit optimistic, because maybe, just maybe, he and I will be able to be friends again someday.

"It's not too late to change your mind about moving," Jade says quietly as her dad pulls in to park in front of her house, where I stayed last night, and I turn her way, feeling my stomach drop when I see sadness in her gaze as her eyes search mine. "But you're not going to, are you?"

"No." I shake my head. "I'm not going to." I reach my hand out to her, and she wraps her pinkie around mine. Over this last month, one of the hardest things I've had to come to terms with is actually leaving the place I've always called home and the people who are my family. But even as difficult as it's been, I know I'm making the right decision for myself, and my life. I know it's going to take time to settle into living with Tanner, and I'm sure that we're both going to have to do a lot of adjusting, but I feel whole when I'm with him, and there's no way I'm going to deny myself that.

"I figured as much." She lets out a deep breath. "I want to be selfish and to tell you that you're making a mistake, but I can't because I can see how much Tanner loves you and know that he'll do everything he can to make you happy. I'm happy for you."

"I love you." My nose stings and my eyes burn.

"I love you too." She looks over at me and sighs. "This isn't even goodbye—I still get to spend the next few days with you."

"I know." I take a deep breath. "I don't know what's wrong with me."

"You're such a girl." She wraps her arm around my shoulders and pulls me into her side. "No crying, or mom will think I'm being mean to you."

"Right." I laugh, remembering when we were younger and how the two of us fighting would normally end up with her in trouble with

Maisie or Bernard; then again, she was the one who typically started the fights between us.

"Are you two ready?" Bernard asks, opening the driver's-side door. "I wanna get a coffee before we head out of town."

"We're ready." Jade lets me go, and we both wheel my suitcases to the back of Bernard's truck, then load up the few boxes I packed and get in. After stopping for coffee and some snacks, we hit the road.

Oh God, I'm going to puke. I hold my hand to my forehead as I pray for the nausea to pass.

"Are you feeling sick again?" Jade asks quietly after a few hours, and I slowly turn my head her way, afraid that any sudden movement will cause me to throw up. Since we've been on the road, I've gotten nauseated more than once, but thankfully we've been just about to stop to use the restroom or get gas each time.

"Yeah." I turn one of the air vents my way, hoping the cool air will help.

"I've never known you to get carsick."

"I haven't before. I probably caught a bug after all the stress from moving."

"Yeah, maybe," she agrees, then mutters, "or maybe you're pregnant."

"Don't say that," I hiss. My heart starts to hammer away inside my chest, because I thought the same thing after I realized I haven't gotten my period yet—something I normally would have gotten a week ago. I glance toward the front seat, thankful that Maisie is asleep and Bernard is distracted by singing along to the radio.

You're on birth control. You can't be pregnant, I remind myself.

"I'm not pregnant."

"Okay," she says, not sounding convinced. "Do you want Dad to stop at the next rest stop? Maybe if you get out and walk around, you'll feel a little better."

"No," I reply. "We're so close." I glance at the GPS. "I should be able to hold out another hour."

"Are you sure?"

No.

"Yeah." I rest my forehead against the cool glass and watch the forest off the side of the road pass in a blur of green and brown, then close my eyes when it becomes too much.

"Cybil." I blink my eyes open and find Maisie turned around toward me, and I sit up as Bernard pulls in to park in front of Tanner's house. "You fell asleep, sweetheart."

"Not sleeping much last night must have caught up with me." I yawn as I grab my cell phone. "I was supposed to call Tanner to let him know when we were thirty minutes out so that he could come meet us. We'll probably have to wait a few minutes for him to get here."

"That's fine." She unhooks her belt and hops out, stretching her arms over her head while I put my cell to my ear.

"Hey, sunshine, are you close?" Tanner greets, sounding happy, and I smile.

"Actually, we're already here. I fell asleep. I'm sorry."

"No big deal. There's a key in a rock in the garden next to the front step. You can use that to get in, and I'll be there in about twenty minutes, tops."

"All right." I unhook my belt and open my door.

"Fuck, I can't wait to kiss you."

"Me too." My heart flutters.

"I'm getting in my truck. I'll see you in a few minutes."

"See you in a few," I say. Then I whisper, "Love you."

"I love you too." He hangs up, and I hop down out of my seat and walk to where Maisie, Bernard, and Jade are standing.

"Tanner said there's a rock near the steps with a key in it," I tell them, and Maisie turns to look at me. I notice her eyes are glistening. "What happened? Are you okay?"

"This looks almost exactly like your mom's house." She walks toward me and wraps me in a tight hug, whispering, "It's like serendipity, being here and knowing this is going to be where you'll live and start a family of your own."

I squeeze my eyes closed, not wanting to cry. What the hell is wrong with me? I've never been this emotional. Clearing my throat, I smile. "I said the same thing when I saw it the first time. I mean, not the part about starting a family here, but that this place is just like Mom's house."

She laughs and lets me go. "There's plenty of time for talk of babies later on."

"Did Tanner say exactly what the rock with the key in it looks like?" Bernard asks, cutting into the moment, and I look to where he's standing and can't help but laugh, because there are dozens of rocks near the bottom step in the garden, on both sides of the stairs.

"He didn't, but if we don't find it, he'll be here in just a few minutes." I go to help him look while Jade and Maisie walk around the house to take in the view.

"Victory!" Bernard exclaims, coming up with the key after a couple of minutes, and I take it from him, unlock the front door, and head inside, with everyone following me.

"There's a bathroom here." I touch the door in the hall where the half bath is, then go toward the kitchen and smile when I see a large bouquet of flowers on the counter with a "Welcome Home" balloon floating in the air above it.

"I'm really trying not to get jealous, but seriously, you have the best luck," Jade says, leaning in to smell one of the red roses. "Not only did you land a hot guy, but you landed a hot guy with a job and a fucking awesome house."

"Language," Maisie says with a sigh, then mutters, "not that I don't agree with you. This place is beautiful." She opens the back door and steps out onto the deck, with Bernard at her back.

"I can see why you said you love his house," Jade says, wandering around the living room.

"There's a lot to love," I agree, but really I would move into a one-room shack, as long as I had Tanner with me.

"Sunshine." Hearing Tanner's voice, I spin around and rush to the front door, launching myself into his arms. As he lifts me off the ground, I wrap my legs around his hips. "Fuck, I missed you." He cups the back of my neck with one hand and pulls my mouth down to his so he can thrust his tongue between my lips. I don't hesitate to open for him, and I swear my soul sighs as his familiar taste, scent, and touch sink into my senses.

When he slows the kiss and pulls back, I grasp his face and whisper against his lips, "I missed you too."

"Tanner's home!" I hear Jade yell to Maisie and Bernard, and Tanner's hand at the back of my neck squeezes. "I think I'm going to need to call the fire department to get the Jaws of Life to separate the two of them."

"I told you she's annoying," I whisper, and he grins as he places me on my feet.

"Hey, Jade," he greets, and I turn to catch her roll her eyes at him before coming over to give him a hug. I stand back and watch them embrace, feeling hopeful that one day they might truly be friends, especially since the two of them mean the world to me. "How was the drive?"

"Beautiful," Maisie says, giving him a hug and a pat on the cheek. "You have a beautiful home."

"Thank you," Tanner says softly as she lets him go.

"I thought Oregon was God's country. Seems I was wrong." Bernard gives him a handshake with one of those manly guy-hugs that includes a pat on the back. "Maisie and I might just have to talk to a real estate agent while we're here."

"Wait, you and Mom would actually consider moving here?" Jade cuts in, sounding horrified, and Maisie grabs her hand.

"Don't worry; we're not moving." She shrugs. "Or at least not until Daddy retires in a couple of years."

"But you love Oregon," Jade says, looking between her parents.

"Who's hungry?" Tanner asks, and I want to kiss him for his interruption. Jade has been having a hard enough time with me moving away. I don't think she would be able to handle her parents even considering moving too.

"I'm starving,"

"You're not feeling sick anymore?" Jade asks, and I feel all eyes come to me.

"You were feeling sick?" Tanner and Maisie ask at the same time.

"I'm fine—I just got carsick a couple of times on the drive." I shrug off their concern. "I'm fine now."

"Are you sure?" Bernard asks, his eyes scanning me in one quick glance.

"I'm sure." I look up at Tanner when his hand grabs hold of mine, seeing worry in his gaze. "I promise I'm fine."

With a nod, he pulls his eyes off me and looks to everyone. "I was thinking we could go to the Edge for dinner. They have good food and a covered patio, so we can eat outside."

"That works," Bernard says. "I just want to get all the bags unpacked before we head out so we won't have to do it later."

"I'll help you." Tanner lets my hand go with a squeeze before he follows Bernard out of the house. With the guys outside unpacking our suitcases, I show Jade and Maisie the two spare rooms with a Jack-and-Jill bathroom between them. When the guys come back in, we all agree to shower or freshen up before we head out to dinner.

Halfway through my shower, Tanner joins me, which means I get a welcome home that involves an orgasm, and we end up taking a little longer to join everyone, but thankfully, no one says anything. Not that I would have cared if they had.

Chapter 24

Cybil

"Morning, sunshine." Tanner's warm lips press against my bare shoulder as his hand curves around my hip, and I turn toward him and burrow my face against his chest, trying to fight back the nausea that's haunted me every morning since I got here.

"Morning." I blink my eyes open and find that he's dressed, in a T-shirt and a pair of cutoff sweats. "Did you already work out?"

"No, not yet, but I have something to show you before everyone else wakes up," he says quietly against my ear, and a shiver runs down my spine as I tip my head back to meet his gaze.

"What is it?"

"You'll see." He smiles, kissing me softly. "Get dressed, and I'll meet you in the kitchen."

"Okay," I agree, watching him get out of bed; then his eyes roam over me, and he shakes his head.

"Have I told you how happy I am to have you home?"

Home . . . yes, I'm home, and that's what it feels like being with him.

"You mentioned it." I can't help my smile, and he places his fists in the bed on either side of my hips.

"Well, I'm really fucking happy." He kisses me swiftly once more, then orders "Get up, babe" before he leaves the room, giving me one last look.

I don't get up immediately. It takes me a few minutes to summon enough energy to sit up, then a few more minutes to actually put my feet on the floor. By the time I do meet him in the kitchen, he's got two tumblers filled with coffee and a smile on his face. "Where are we going?" I ask when he grabs a zip-up hoodie and then helps me into it.

"Do you trust me?"

"You know I do," I say, and he gives me a look that makes me warm all over, zips up the sweatshirt, and kisses my nose.

"Good." He gives me one of the coffees, takes my hand, and walks me out the back door, down the steps, and toward the big metal building behind his house. "Blake, Mav, and Dave helped me with this project when I got home." He looks down at me and lets my hand go so that he can pull a key out of his pocket. "When Janet, Margret, and Cammy heard what we were doing, they wanted to add their touch, and this morning I finished setting up the last piece so I could finally show you." My heart starts to pound as he opens the heavy metal door on the side of the shop, steps inside, and turns on the lights. I follow behind him, and my breath catches as I look around. The space is smaller than my shop back in Oregon, but it's much nicer. Dark wood covers the floors, shelves with pretty floral wallpaper line one of the larger walls, photos I took on my trip here are on the smaller wall, and lots of empty cubbies fill the other side of the room, with a large sewing desk and chair in the middle. "I just wanted you to have a place to work, a space you could call your own."

"Tanner." Tears fill my eyes, and I turn to face him. "This is . . ." I glance around once more. "I don't even know what to say. It's beautiful, so beautiful."

"I know you're giving up a lot to be with me, but I want you to be happy here, baby." He wraps his arms around me, and I tuck my face against his chest.

"I don't need this to be happy, but I love it." I sniffle, feeling his lips at the top of my head. "Thank you." I gaze up at him, and he cups my cheeks. "This is amazing."

"When we get the storage unit built on the lodge property and all the equipment moved out, I'll put in a kitchen and restroom out here and open up the rest of the building so you can use it all."

"You don't have to do that." I look around, picturing all my material and bags filling the space. "This is more than enough."

"That might be, but I'm still going to do it." He watches me walk over to the desk with a smile on his face.

"So how much time do you think we have before everyone wakes up?" I put my hands on the desk, testing how sturdy it is, and the heated look in his eyes makes my nipples hard.

"No one knows where we are." He prowls toward me, lifts me off my feet, sets my bottom on the desk, and covers my mouth with his. It doesn't take long for me to kick off the shorts I have on, and even less time for him to spread my legs and enter me in one hard thrust. Digging my nails into his biceps, I hold on tight as he sends me flying and keep holding on when his thrusts become jerky and he loses himself inside me.

"Are you sure you don't want to come into town with us?" Maisie asks, and I plaster a fake smile on my face.

"Yeah, I just want to get some stuff unpacked and settled in," I tell her, hoping that she doesn't see that I'm lying.

"Okay, well, I have my phone; call if you want us to bring you anything."

"Sure." I accept a kiss to my cheek from her and ignore the look that Jade gives me. As my best friend, I know she knows something isn't right, but I'm thankful that she hasn't confronted me. That said, I know she wants to; we just haven't had time alone for her to do it. "You guys have fun, and you should totally go to the Root for lunch."

"We might do that." Maisie grabs her bag while Jade picks up hers. "We'll be out in a couple hours."

"I'll be here." I walk them to the door and wave them off before heading to the bedroom and changing out of my shorts and into a pair of jeans.

With Tanner and Bernard fishing and Jade and Maisie out exploring town, I know this might be the only moment I have alone for the next few days. After I slip on a pair of flip-flops, I grab my keys off the hook near the front door and leave the house, making a beeline for my Bronco.

Once inside, I start the engine and take comfort in the smell of the interior that reminds me of my mom before I put the gearshift into drive. I turn onto the main road into town, trying not to freak myself out, even though I'm already freaked out. My period is late, and every day, I've woken up more tired than I was the night before when I went to sleep, feeling nauseous. Always nauseous.

Thankfully, no one else has noticed (or no one has said anything), but if I'm right and I'm pregnant, I won't be able to hide what's going on for very long. When I get to Target, I head inside, not even bothering to look around, which is something I would normally do. Instead, I go straight for the pregnancy tests, and since there are so many brands, all of them proclaiming different results, I decide to grab a few.

With my hands full, I start for the checkout but stop dead when I hear a voice nearby that sends a shiver down my spine. With my heart suddenly pounding, I tiptoe to the end of the aisle and look around the corner. Standing just feet away is a man with a cart, while the woman he's with searches through a bin in the middle of the aisle. As I study him, my heart feels like it's going to come out of my chest.

Because without a doubt, he's one of the men I saw in the woods weeks ago.

One of the men who killed the elk and then shot at Tanner and me.

As if he senses me, his head lifts, and his eyes meet mine.

"Shit," I hear him say, and without thinking, I take off, still carrying an armful of pregnancy tests. When I hear his feet pounding the ground behind me, I run faster and head right for the automatic doors and out, ignoring the alarms going off as I run outside.

"Stop!" I hear someone shout, and tears fill my eyes as I book it toward my Bronco. When I finally reach my door, I fumble with the handle, the tests in my hands falling to the ground while someone crashes into me from behind. The impact causes the air in my lungs to leave on a whoosh.

"I won't tell anyone I saw you. I swear I won't tell!" I scream as I spin around, ready to fight to the death if I have to.

"I don't know what you're talking about, but the cops are on the way," a kid younger than me, wearing a red polo shirt, says and then grabs my upper arm.

I blink. "What?" I pant for breath, scanning the area for the guy who I swear was chasing me.

"The cops are coming," he says again as I hear the sound of sirens getting closer.

"I . . . I thought—"

"You have to come with me." He latches onto my wrist, then bends to pick up the boxes on the ground at our feet.

"This is a mistake. I didn't try to steal those. I . . . there was a guy chasing me."

"Yeah, I was chasing you." He drags me back into the store and into a small office where there are dozens of TV monitors lining the walls.

Chapter 25

Tanner

With Bernard at my back, I head into the lodge so I can show him around, even though I'm ready to be home with Cybil after spending the day on the river fishing with him. Cybil said I shouldn't bring up him and Maisie moving here, but after having them around this last week and seeing how happy she's been, I've made a point to show all of them everything this area has to offer. I'm also hoping that if they decide to move this way, Jade will follow.

"Gotta say I'm impressed, son," Bernard says as we step into the great room in the center of the lodge. "You and your friends have done good for yourselves."

"Thanks," I say as my cell phone in my pocket rings. When I pull it out, a number I don't recognize is on the screen. Not sure if it's a client, I put it to my ear. "Hello?"

"Is this Tanner Carson?"

"It is." I meet Bernard's gaze, and he raises a brow.

"This is Officer Thomas Swans. I'm sorry to call you, but I have a woman with me who asked that I phone you before I take her down to the station—"

"Cybil?" I cut him off as I start moving toward the front door of the lodge, swearing I hear someone crying in the background.

"Yes, she said you'd be able to explain why she tried to steal four pregnancy tests."

I stumble and just catch myself by latching onto the railing before I can fall down the steps outside the lodge. "What?"

"Sorry, she's very incoherent. She also said something about a shooting and an elk."

"Where is she?" I bark into the phone as I run toward my truck, hoping Bernard is keeping up, because if not, he's going to get left behind.

"We're in the Target parking lot."

"Do not leave."

"Sir, I can't—"

"She must have seen the person who shot at us, the person who poached an elk almost two months ago. Call the sheriff and warden. They'll confirm my story."

"Fuck," he mutters before sighing. "All right."

"I'll be there in twenty, tops. Please don't leave." I hang up as I start the engine of my truck.

"What's going on?" Bernard asks, and I grit my teeth. I forgot he was here. *Fuck.*

Not wanting to repeat what the cop said about Cybil trying to steal pregnancy tests, I tell him a half truth. "I think Cybil saw the person who shot at us, and she's with the cops."

He doesn't say a word, and I'm thankful for the silence as I drive, because my mind is whirling with thoughts of Cybil pregnant with our child and scared out of her mind in the back seat of a cop car.

When we pull into the Target parking lot, it takes less than two seconds to spot Cybil. She's not in the back of a cruiser but instead being held under the arm of the sheriff who spoke to her the night we were shot at. I don't even bother finding a parking spot. I pull up right in front of the line of official vehicles outside the store and somehow manage to shut down the engine of my truck before I hop out and run around the hood. When Cybil sees me, her eyes fill with concern and relief.

"Sunshine," I say low, and she rushes toward me as I open my arms. As soon as I have hold of her, she sobs, gripping onto my tee. "Shhh, it's okay." I rock her back and forth, then look over the top of her head as the sheriff walks toward us.

"Security's going over the tapes with a couple of officers. We're hoping we got the man who shot at the two of you on tape." The sheriff's eyes drop to Cybil. "You should probably get her home. We'll call and let you know when we find something."

"Thanks." I turn to lead her to my truck and see Bernard a couple of feet away. "Sunshine, did you drive here?" When she nods, I take her purse off her shoulder and look at Bernard. "Do you mind driving Cybil's Bronco home?"

"Not at all." He takes her bag when I hand it over and digs through for her keys. Once he has them, he hands me her purse and looks at Cybil as she wipes her cheeks. "Are you okay, honey?"

"Yeah," she mumbles, and even though he doesn't look convinced, he lets it go and mutters that he'll follow us back to the house.

I usher Cybil to my truck and place her in the passenger seat, making sure to take extra care when I buckle her in while ignoring her body stiffening when my knuckles graze her stomach.

"Talk to me, sunshine," I whisper after I get in behind the wheel and grab her hand.

"I heard the cop talking to you. I know you know about the pregnancy tests."

"Are you pregnant?" I ask, the idea thrilling and scaring the shit out of me.

"I don't know," she says, sounding so defeated. "Probably. My period is late, and I've been feeling sick every morning and so tired all the time."

"I wish you would have told me."

"I was going to if I found out I was."

I smile at the anger in her tone. "I know you would have, but you're not alone, sunshine. I'm here with you no matter what."

"I know." She starts to fiddle with my fingers.

"Whatever happens, we will work through it." I lift her hand to my lips, kissing her fingers. "Okay?"

"Okay," she agrees before resting her head on my shoulder.

For the rest of the drive home, I don't say anything, and when we get back to the house, I lead her to the bedroom and order her to lie down and take a nap. Surprisingly, she doesn't fight me, or maybe she's so exhausted she can't.

Two hours later, with Maisie and Jade back at the house and Bernard on edge, the sheriff calls to say he's going to stop by with a few pictures for her to look at, which means I have to wake her up.

I hold her hand as he shows her pictures of the man from the Target footage, a man who did chase after her as she ran from the store, and a man the cops know, judging by the mug shots they have of him. They also show her the photos of two other men he was closely associated with, and after she confirms they're the men who were with him that day, the sheriff assures us that the three of them will soon be dealt with.

After the sheriff leaves, Maisie and Jade take Cybil outside to the back deck, and the three of them curl up on the couch to watch a movie, while Bernard sprawls out in the living room with a beer in front of the TV.

Knowing everyone needs to eat, I gather orders and head into town to pick up dinner from a local Chinese place and stop at a drugstore to buy a couple of pregnancy tests. It's obvious that Cybil has been worried about possibly being pregnant, and I want her to know that we're a team, no matter what happens. When I get home, I place the tests in the bathroom, then sit down with everyone to eat dinner. By the time we're all ready for bed, Cybil is exhausted, and I don't blame her—it's been a very busy day, with lots of excitement.

"You bought tests?" She picks up one of the boxes off the counter and flips it over to read the back.

"You don't have to take it now." I wrap my arms around her from behind and rest my jaw against the side of her head. "But before you take it, sunshine, I want you to know that a positive or negative result doesn't change anything. Okay?"

"Okay," she agrees, and I kiss her cheek. She steps away from me without another word, then heads into the room where the toilet is. A few minutes later, when she comes out, she sets the test on top of the box on the counter, then washes her hands. "We have to wait three minutes."

"Come here," I order, dragging her toward me and holding her against my chest. As I watch the time on the clock tick away, a sense of hopefulness comes over me. I've never really put much consideration into my future or what it might look like, but with Cybil in my life, I'm looking forward to making her my wife, starting a family together—whether that happens now or down the road—and becoming the best father I can be. I might not have had the best examples growing up, but I do know I want to be better than my parents were, and I have no doubt the people who love me now will help if I ever need it.

"The time's up," she says quietly, tucking her face against my chest while wrapping her arms around my waist. "You look."

My heart pounds like it's trying to escape my chest as I reach around her to pick up the thin piece of plastic and see the large plus sign on the screen.

"Tanner."

"We're having a baby." I grasp her tightly and drop my lips to the top of her head, completely overwhelmed by the idea of our baby, *my* baby, growing inside her.

"I'm pregnant?" Her whispered question is filled with awe, and I drop to my knees in front of her and lift the tank top she went to sleep in last night.

"Marry me." I look up at her, watching her eyes fill with tears.

"Tanner, you don't have to—"

"Stop," I growl, cutting her off before she can piss me off by saying something ridiculous like I don't have to marry her just because she's pregnant with my child. "I love you. I want to spend forever with you."

I place a kiss against her flat stomach, then stand up and grab her hand to lead her from the bathroom into the closet. I let her hand go so I can grab a bag from one of the high shelves and then dig into it until I find the box I'm looking for.

"The day I got back home from Oregon, I went to a local jeweler and picked this out for you." I open the box, and her eyes widen. "Even before that, I knew I would ask you to be my wife, ask you to share your life with me."

"Tanner." Her fingers cover her lips.

"I love you, sunshine. You're the best thing to ever happen to me, and I want to spend the rest of my life with you."

"Okay," she says quietly, fingering the ring in the box before meeting my gaze.

"So you'll marry me?"

"Yes." She nods, her eyes shining with unshed tears.

"Thank fuck." I slide the ring onto her finger, then curl my arms around her.

"I love you."

"I love you too." I grasp her face and tip her head back so I can kiss her. "I promise I'll do everything in my power to make sure you're happy, baby."

"You already make me happier than I've ever been." She leans up on her tiptoes while grasping on to my shirt, and I drop my face down to hers and groan as her tongue touches my bottom lip.

As I take over the kiss, I lead her back into the bedroom, then take my time stripping her out of her tank top and panties. Once she's laid out for me, her hair spilling across my pillows, her lips swollen, her nipples harden and the space between her legs becomes wet. I make love to her, understanding for the first time in my life what love, real love, really is.

And after we've both finished and she's fallen asleep, I hold my hand against her stomach, promising my child that I'll do everything within my power to make sure that he or she and their mother are always happy.

Epilogue

Cybil

I pull up and park in front of the lodge and unhook my seat belt before grabbing my purse from the passenger seat. It takes me a minute to maneuver myself and my giant belly out from behind the steering wheel, but I manage with only a little huffing and puffing. Once my feet are on the ground, I slam the door and head up the stairs toward the front door, smiling when Janet steps outside to greet me with a warm hug and a wide smile. The moment reminds me of the day Tanner and I got married six months ago here at the lodge.

"Look at how beautiful you are." She takes a moment to rub my belly. The belly rubbing is something that has definitely taken some getting used to. "How is she doing?"

"He's good, healthy, normal." I listen to her laugh as I rest my hand on my eight-month bump. Tanner and I decided that we would wait until our baby was born to find out the sex, but that doesn't mean everyone doesn't have a preference. I for one want a boy who looks like his daddy, while Tanner wants a little girl. More than anything, we just want him or her to be healthy.

"Tanner and Mav are in the office with Everly." She opens the door for me, and I slip off my jacket. A couple of months ago, Tanner, Mav, and Blake all agreed that they needed to hire someone to help run the office, especially with Tanner wanting to take some time off to be home with the baby and me after I give birth. But even with them all agreeing, Blake dragged his feet on actually choosing someone, so Mav took it upon himself to hire Everly, a cute little brunette with a ten-month-old son who just moved to town.

"How's that going—is Blake coming around to the idea of having Everly around?" I ask, following her through the lodge.

"Blake is avoiding the office and Everly as much as possible." She gives me a look over her shoulder with a knowing glint in her eyes, and I laugh.

"I thought I heard your laugh." Tanner steps out of the office and makes a beeline for me. "Hey, sunshine."

"Hey." I lean up for a kiss when he bends down to brush his lips across mine.

"How are my girls today?" he asks while palming my belly.

"Me and your son are good," I say with a smile, and he chuckles.

"I was just about to make some lunch—are you hungry?" Janet asks, and I shake my head.

"No, thank you—I ate before I drove down," I tell her, and she nods.

"I'll be in the kitchen. Come visit with me before you take off."

"I will," I promise, and she smiles at Tanner before wandering off down the hall. Once she's out of sight, Tanner slides his hand up my back, and I turn to focus on him.

"Did you drive the Subaru?" he asks, and my nose scrunches. About a month after we confirmed that I was pregnant, he bought me a brand-new Subaru, insisting that it's safer than my Bronco, but I've only driven it a handful of times, something that I know annoys him greatly. "Baby."

"I like my car."

"I know you do, and I understand why, but it's not safe for you and our baby to be in your car."

"It's fine."

"It's not." He gives me a look that says clearly he's not happy. "If something was to happen to you, I couldn't—" His jaw clenches as he cuts off his statement, and my stomach twists because I know that's his worst fear, and I get it because I don't know what I would do if something were to happen to him.

"Okay," I say softly, resting my palm against his chest and feeling his heart thumping hard. This isn't our first conversation on this subject, but I've never seen real worry from him about it until now. "I'll drive the Subaru from now on."

"Promise?" His eyes search mine, and I nod. "Thank you, sunshine." He wraps his hand around the nape of my neck, then touches his lips to mine. When he pulls away, his eyes go over the top of my head. I look to see what or who has caught his attention and see Blake standing a few feet away.

"Cybil." Blake comes to greet me; then, like he's done for a while now, he places a kiss on my cheek. "How's my nephew?" His eyes drop to my stomach.

"Good, active—especially when I want to sleep," I tell him, and his eyes soften.

"Not much longer and he'll be keeping you up all night like Taylor's doing to Margret," he says with a warm smile, referring to his sister's newborn daughter, Taylor, who's already crawling around and giving Margret a run for her money.

"I can't wait until he's here so they can entertain each other," I say, and Tanner cuts in.

"You two really need to stop referring to my daughter as a boy."

"He is a boy." I turn to grin at him as I rest my hand on my stomach.

"She's not," he denies, then looks at Blake when he chuckles. "Everything okay?"

"Yep, just need to get the guest list printed so we're ready for tomorrow," Blake tells him, looking toward the closed office door.

"Everly already took care of it," Tanner tells him, and instead of looking impressed, Blake looks annoyed.

"Right, then I'm going to—"

His words are cut off when pain slices through my stomach and back, and I reach out and dig my nails into his bicep and cling to Tanner's shirt so that I don't fall to my knees.

"Sunshine." Tanner's panicked voice cuts through the fog of pain, and I take a deep breath. "What is it?"

"I don't know," I answer once I'm able; then I meet his worried gaze as my heart starts to race. "It's too early for me to go into labor, right?"

"You think you're in labor?"

"I don't know." I hold my stomach, which feels tight. "I think so." Tears fill my eyes because something isn't right.

"It'll be okay." He scoops me up and heads toward the front of the lodge, with Blake right behind us. Before I can say a word, the two of them get me into Tanner's truck, and the next thing I know, I'm being admitted to the hospital.

~

Tanner

Dressed in a set of scrubs, I follow a nurse into the operating room, and my heart seizes in my chest when I see Cybil lying on the hospital bed attached to machines, with a large blue sheet blocking my view of her belly. Her belly where our baby has been growing for months; her belly that I've kissed, rubbed, and fallen in love with. When I meet her worried gaze, I attempt to hide the fear I'm feeling; she doesn't need to know that I'm scared, but I am. Other than a little bit of morning sickness, her pregnancy has been easy, so finding out after they ran some tests that she's suffering from placental abruption has been a shock for both of us.

"You have to stay right next to her head," the nurse informs me. I lift my chin, letting her know that I heard her, then walk toward my wife.

"Hey, sunshine." I smooth my hand over the top of her hair, and tears fill her beautiful eyes. "It's going to be okay," I assure her, praying that I'm right.

"I'm so scared, Tanner."

"I know, baby." I drop my forehead to rest against hers and whisper soothing nonsense as the doctors and nurses work around us. Time seems to go in slow motion, and I don't even think I really breathe until a sharp cry fills the room over the sound of quiet murmurs.

"Mom and Dad, you have a beautiful, healthy little girl," a woman announces, and tears I can't hold back fill my eyes as I wipe away the tracks of tears from Cybil's temples.

"You were right," Cybil whispers, sounding tired but happy, and I press my lips to her forehead, holding them there as a whirlwind of activity begins to swarm around us.

"So proud of you, baby."

"You always say that." I see her smile through the mask she has on before I turn to watch a group of nurses clean up our girl and check her over. "Is she okay? What does she look like?"

"She's okay, she's beautiful," I assure her, then focus on her beautiful sleepy face. "We still need to decide on her name."

"Claire Montana after my mom and the place we fell in love," she says, her eyes searching mine and looking unsure, and I rest my lips against her forehead.

"I love it, and you." I smooth my hand over her hair.

"Here she is, Mom and Dad," a nurse says, quietly holding Claire close to Cybil's chest, and I reach out and carefully touch her cheek with the tip of my finger.

"She's perfect." I look at my two girls, not sure that I'll ever get used to loving two people so much. Before Cybil, I had no idea what love was, and now with our daughter here with us, I'm sure I didn't.

~

Cybil

"I love you," I whisper to my husband, watching him hold Claire's tiny body against his bare chest, and he turns his head my way, giving me a warm smile filled with contentment and happiness.

"I love you, too, sunshine." He reaches across the space between us and touches my cheek. "I love both my girls." He kisses the top of Claire's head, and tears fill my eyes.

I'm sure some people might think I rushed into love, but without a doubt it was the best thing I've ever done, and I truly believe that my mom had something to do with the miracle I was given.